The Stone Collection

The Stone Collection

Kateri Akiwenzie-Damm

HIGHWATER PRESS

HighWater Press is an imprint of Portage & Main Press.

Printed and bound in Canada by Friesens

Design by Mike Carroll

Print ISBN: 978-1-55379-549-0
Digital ISBN: 978-1-55379-596-4

LIBRARY AND ARCHIVES CANADA CATALOGUING IN PUBLICATION

Akiwenzie-Damm, Kateri, 1965-, author
     The stone collection / Kateri Akiwenzie-Damm.

Short stories.
ISBN 978-1-55379-549-0 (paperback)

     I. Title.

PS8557.A495S76 2015   C813'.54   C2015-905704-3

HighWater Press gratefully acknowledges for their financial support the Government of Canada through the Canada Book Fund, the Canada Council for the Arts, the Manitoba Book Publishing Tax Credit, and the Manitoba Department of Culture, Heritage, & Tourism.

THE DEBWE SERIES

Exceptional Indigenous Writing from Across Canada

HIGHWATER
PRESS

Toll-Free: 1-800-667-9673
www.highwaterpress.com

For my beautiful sons Kegedonce and Gaadoohn. I love you every minute of every day, all the time, no matter what.

For my boy Theo and for Teddy and all Indigenous babies and children hurt while in the care of Child and Family Services.

For Michael Akiwenzie and all of the other children who entered the Indian Residential School system and never made it home again.

For all of the missing and murdered Indigenous women in Canada.

We remember.

stone song

like stones are alive
like stones dream stillness
like stones are alive
like stones hold energy
like stones are alive
like stones store history
like stones are alive
like stones hold story
like stones are alive
like stones dream winter
like stones are alive
like stones are alive
like stones are alive

you are the earth in winter

CONTENTS

PICKING STONES

YOU RIDE BIKES PAST THE LUMBER MILL TO A SHELTERED BEACH.
Leaving your bikes you walk, finding a large piece of driftwood to
shelter you from the wind. The wind is steady. Riding there she
pointed out spots of interest, spinning small webs of understanding for you. You watched intently. Sometimes you just watched
her, concentrating so seriously on her that you lost track of what
she was saying. She is one of those people whose movements
speak very strongly, very clearly even when you aren't yet capable
of fully understanding. So without forethought your mind locks
on what she is doing, the way the muscles in her legs propel the
bicycle forward, the way her hands grip the handlebars, the way
her lips form each word, the way she exerts a steady, silent presence in the pauses. Her words slip past you sometimes, taken
whizzing past your ears by the wind. And somehow it's okay.

It's okay even though what you do hear knocks you on the skull.

As you rode your leg muscles began to twitch and your breath began to grow ragged around the edges. Then you noticed with some embarrassment that she continued to talk evenly, peddling with an easy rhythm despite the many more years she has weathered. You secretly blamed the wind, the borrowed bicycle, your fear of testing the gears, but you continued watching, listening, and propelling the bicycle with your legs. You continued to concentrate on her and began to suspect that there is some other form of communication occurring between you. Some form of communication that you are only vaguely aware of and that you have never experienced before.

Now in front of the driftwood you sit and talk. You pick at rocks and shells. Examining them, replacing most, pocketing a couple. One that is typical of the rest, that will remind you of the place, the people, the talk. One that is special, that will remind you of the beauty you found hidden in certain people, places, words. Then you stretch out on your side, listening, soaking in the place, her presence, still looking at bits of the shore as she tells you some small fragments of what she knows. And the stones are like stories piling on the shore of memory.

The lumber mill has ripped the face off the hill.

The people allow it in exchange for money and, in the past, a few jobs, she tells you.

But the jobs, like eroding pieces of the hill, are gone now. Still the money allows them to keep the land, that's what they say. The land that is slowly falling into the sea.

Easy for you, you have good-paying jobs, they say. And there is no easy response. So the hill is sacrificed bit by bit for now in the hopes the people will have a future. Easy for the lumber mill. Difficult for everyone else.

You rise together and walk. The shore, as far as you can see, is covered in stones. You imagine each one is a story she has told to other listeners on other bike rides, other walks. Then stopping, stooping, you scoop up a handful of stones, pebbles, shells. As you let them sift through your fingers, you notice one, a little different from the rest. You notice its texture, imagining the layers of silt that have combined with incredible forces of energy to form this solid piece of earth. You notice how the movement of the waves has worn the rough edges smooth, how the stone is solid in your hand and soft against your skin. Clutching it in your palm, you feel its energy pulsing into your flesh, and it becomes part of your memory, your mind memory, skin memory, muscle memory.

You skip along the stones knowing without looking that she is just ahead of you and to the left, waiting. She jumps onto a rock to scan below the surface while you catch up. Just as you reach her you stop and dip your hand into a little pool along the shore. Is it cold? You wiggle your fingers then look up. Yeah. But not enough to make your bones ache. You add that last bit with just a hint of bravado. Wouldn't want to go for a swim though. You both smile.

You jump up on the rock, and the two of you stand together. The sea isn't yielding what she wanted to show, so she continues walking, and you follow. She picks up a plastic shampoo container washed up on the rocks. Japanese, she says. Those boats are supposed to stay 200 kilometres offshore. You glance at the container, noticing the foreign script. Later you come across a rusting oil drum. You both stop and look at it, saying little. She sets the shampoo container down eventually as you walk.

At a small pile of oval whitish rocks you stop. You pick one up. It's lighter than expected. She turns and watches.

Pumice.

You nod, rubbing your finger against it.

You can use it to rub away dried skin, calluses. Again you nod. Do you have it where you're from? she asks.

Nah, we have to buy it.

It's lava rock. Take some, she says simply.

Okay, you agree, bending over and selecting a smaller-size stone that you stuff into a pocket with the other stones you have collected.

And so you walk along, talking, stopping to look at stones, birds, a beached buoy, shells. You walk along chatting easily, sometimes saying nothing. And the silence is light and easy between you.

It's Not So Much

IT'S NOT SO MUCH BEING DEAD HE MINDS, IT'S THE WAY IT happened, he likes to tell the other Invisibles.

What freakin' difference does that make? Tony would always ask. You're dead! He's always a real smartass like that.

Then Kowhai or one of the others would tell Tony to shut up, and a big argument would break out. Good thing Invisibles are also Unhearables, I tell them, what with all that racket going on all the time. Sometimes though I wish some of my friends could hear them too. Some of it's pretty funny. Some of it makes those little hairs on the back of my neck rise like little ghosts. Those Invisibles have seen some crazy stuff, and they just love to talk about it.

Like take Jervis. Always on about the way he died. Made my skin crawl the first few times I heard it. The first time I heard him I went to talk to my Mishomis.

He was sitting on a tree stump outside the old place. Ahnee, I say to him.

Ahnee, he says back. Then he points his lip at the blue-and-white nylon lawn chair beside him. So I sit down. It was one of those grey November days. The ones where it snows, and it seems like the whole world is melting just like the snow is melting, and everything is damp and cold. Together we watched the snow turn to small grains of ice falling from the sky.

aHmmm, I say to him.

Ya know, he says, it's not so much the cold, it's the dampness.

Yeah. I wrap my arms around myself. Wasn't so damp last night, I say. He doesn't say anything. So I say, I was sitting there in my room, and that door opened, and I could hear footsteps, but no one was there. Was pretty cold though, eh. He looked at his hands, so I went on. Yeah, so anyway I can't really see him, but I know someone's standing there beside me like he's just waiting, so I say to him, hey, whaddaya want?

I blow on my fingers and hunch my shoulders to keep warm. I clear my throat before I continue.

I don't hear anything at first. Then I hear kind of a buzzing like there's a fly trapped in my ear, moving down my ear canal. Then I hear this guy yell, how about now? Can you hear me now?!

Just about jumped through the ceiling. Geez, I say, ya don't haveta yell. You're new at this, hey? Ya scared the crap outta me.

He told me his name was Jervis. So I said, Jervis, buddy, you're dead. And he said, Yeah. He said it wasn't so much being dead he minded, it was the way it happened.

Mishomis stares at the trees across the road. So I stare at them too.

Got a smoke? he asks after we've been staring for a while. I'm not supposed to smoke, but I pull out my pack, hand him a smoke, and take out one for myself. I take out my Bic in that beaded case

Pechi made for me when she liked me, and I lean over to light his cigarette first. Mishomis sucks his cheeks in so far I swear they musta hit each other inside his mouth. But I don't say anything. I just light my smoke.

He blows the smoke out real slow, real long. Like I think he's gonna pass out or that his lung's gonna collapse or something. Real slow. And just staring across the road the whole time.

I blow smoke rings for a while. By now we're covered in a thin film of ice and I'm starting to shiver. It really is the dampness, not the cold that soaks into your bones.

We both stare at the horizon, that old man and me. The sky is that strange translucent grey-white colour it gets in November. The maple trees across the road are bare, poking their scrawny fingers at the navels of clouds. In the distance the escarpment looms, one of four limestone warriors protecting the land, the people, and the sapphire bay curving around our peninsula. There's not a bird above us, not a bird in those bony trees, not a sound except the sound of my breathing. Mishomis is blowing cigarette smoke at the sky.

So, I say.

He shrugs. One time when your Gramma was visiting her sister someone sat in the rocking chair by the fire all night. Mighta been that uncle she inherited the chair from when her mom died. Maybe. He inhales slightly then exhales real slow again. Said he'd been trying to walk home from one of them residential schools. No boots, no warm clothes. He's shaking so bad he falls down; after a while he stops shaking, and he falls asleep. He said it was the wind, and the damp. Mishomis takes four big drags from his cigarette and blows it towards the tops of the trees. Then he sits there looking at the sleet dropping onto the dry leaves that stretch from his feet to the maple trees and disappear over the edge of the escarpment. I put out my cigarette butt with my fingers and place it on the cold ground at my feet, covering it with a few dried pieces of leaves and grass.

That tobacco ain't jus' for blowing smoke rings, he says.

———

That Jervis can be a real pain in the ass.

Comes running into the house, yelling like a crazy person. They found him! They found him! Who, I say. Geez, Jervis, who? Suddenly I'm outside, it's drizzling, and I'm walking down a road. I can hear tree branches rattling. Then there are lights shining in my eyes. Next thing I know I'm in an old shed. It's pitch black except for a bit of moonlight falling through where some boards fell off near the roof. Look at the truck, I hear, but I can't see whoever's saying it. All right. All right, I say. Ever pushy! Then I'm staring at a truck bumper, and there's a dent and scratches in it. A shiver runs from my tailbone up to the base of my skull. Next thing I know I'm staring at an outhouse. Then a rock.

Mom gives me a funny look at breakfast. I'm reading the back of the Cocoa Krispies box. This is crap, I say. Pure crap! We shouldn't have this stuff in the house. Mom raises an eyebrow. Well, I say, it is. We should eat porridge. Dad walks over, grabs my bowl of cereal and the box of Cocoa Krispies, marches past Mom, and flings it all out the patio door.

Hey! I say.

Mom and Dad are wiggling their eyebrows and pursing their lips at each other, and their eyes shimmer like moonlight on the bay.

Hey, I say. I was eating those!

Later Mom asks me what's wrong. Well, actually she said, "Who shit in your Shreddies?" but that's what she meant.

That damn Jervis, I say.

How is he? she asks.

Dragged me all over the place last night, I say, and I tell her about my dream.

Hmmm... she says. What was it you saw at the end?

Some stupid outhouse, I say.

A what? she says.

You know, an outhouse. She looks at me like I'm speaking Chinese or something. A toilet, a privy, a.... a john! I say real exasperated like.

Oh, she says and grins.

And then a small rock, I say.

A what? she says.

A what? Am I speaking English, 'cause I'm starting to wonder. A rock, I say sighing. You know, a rock? One of those hard things Jack's head is filled with?

She gives me a blank look like I'm speaking Tibetan or something.

A rock, a little rock... you know, a small, little rock....

More blank stares. A big pebble, a small boulder, a... a stone, I blurt.

Oh, she says and grins again.

Oh, now you get it, I say real sarcastically, because hey, I'm a 17-year-old guy, and sarcasm and silence are what we do best in these situations.

A john and a stone, I repeat, emphasizing the words *john* and *stone*. She puts her hand in front of her mouth and giggles.

Ha-ha, I say, very funny. I try to say it real angry, but I feel like an idiot.

Hey, says Dad.

I look at him. He's kneeling in front of the woodstove placing wood in as if he's building a house of cards. Careful. I go over and sit in the rocking chair.

That brother of yours is pretty smart, he says.

A smart ass, I almost say, but I don't. Dad doesn't like it when I call my younger brother names. Guess so, I say.

Taught himself how to make elm bark baskets after we saw them ones in Saratoga last year. Coming back from that Leonard Peltier march.

Yeah, I say. But bark ones don't last. He should make them out of old plastic pop bottles or ice cream tubs. Recycle and all that. That'd be smart.

Hmmm... says Dad.

And they'd last, I say.

He strikes a match, and smoke rises from the centre of the wood pile. He blows on it, and it crackles and flares.

Nothing lasts, he says.

The fire is spreading, and we watch it licking at the kindling and moving to the larger blocks of cordwood.

You better bring in some more wood, son. Gonna get our first winter storm tonight.

Okay, I say, and I stand up. How can you tell? I ask him.

Tell what? he says.

That it's gonna storm.

Oh, he says, that. See that window there? he asks, nodding his head to the side.

Yeah, I say, and I go over and look at the sky. It's darkening, and I can see swirling grey clouds moving towards us from across the bay. Oh, I say.

Yeah, he says, now turn to your left. More…more, okay, stop.
Now I'm staring at the TV. Weather report comes on every 30
minutes, he says.

I sigh. Being Anishinaabe is to be surrounded by jokers. A
regular laugh a minute.

Hey, says my dad.

I look at him.

If you see a cereal bowl out there bring it in. He looks at me.
For the porridge tomorrow.

Okay, I say, and I sigh right at him.

Hey, says my dad.

I look at him.

Tobacco is one of the gifts from the Creator.

I hang my head. Maybe I turn red. I'm not sure if it's notice-
able but my ears and cheeks feel burning hot. How did he know?
I'm thinking.

Maybe I could smell smoke on you, Dad says, which makes
my forehead turn hot too. I feel like I was standing there in my
underwear, and now they've just fallen around my ankles.

Or maybe it came to me in a dream, maybe you act like someone who's been doing something he knows he shouldn't, or maybe
your grandpa told me….

I shift from one foot to another. I want to say, But Mishomis
was smoking too! But I don't.

Or maybe when I was walking back from cutting wood up on
the bluff I saw you.

Shit, says Tony, you a jerk or what? Sits right out where anyone can see him, blowing smoke rings.

Yeah, says Jervis, you really should be more careful.

Look who's talking, says Tony.

Leave him alone! says Kowhai. You're such eggs.

Yeah, says Nani, grow up. He's trying to talk to his dad.

What? says Tony. It's true. One's just about as smart as the other. Shit. Right out in the open where anyone can see.

That starts an even bigger argument, and soon they're all yelling about how dumb I was. Like was I really incredibly dumb or just dumb enough to do something stupid once in a while. And they shout examples of my stupidity at each other to support their positions.

Oh, just shut up about it, would ya! I finally say. Can't I do anything without you watching?

Hey, says my dad. And he turns and stares at me. He raises his eyebrows and crosses his arms across his puffed-out chest. He looks like a wrestler.

Jervis...Jervis and them, I say. Not you, Dad. And I pull on my gloves so fast I look like O.J. Simpson struggling to make my own gloves fit. Better get that wood, I say. My ears and cheeks are on fire.

Jervis, Tony, Kowhai, and Nani laugh all the way out to the woodpile.

Jerks.

———

I had a girlfriend too, says Jervis out of the blue. Then he pops a picture of her into my head so I nearly drive the truck off the road, and Jack says, and I quote, Hey, perhaps I should assume control of this vehicle.

You drive? You don't even have a license, I say.

True. However, at least I am capable of driving straight on a straight road, he says.

I scowl at him.

Pretty, hunh? says Jervis. I don't answer him.

Mistake. He flashes her picture in front of my eyes again for longer this time.

Geez! I yell, waving my arm in front of my face.

Hoh-laaay! says Jack, as we zigzag on and off the road. Jervis?
I pull over and let Jack drive. Take the back way, I tell him.
There're nothing but back ways, he says.
Whatever.
He puts his pow wow CD in the stereo. I get to select the music
since I'm driving he says. There's not much I can say since I made
the rule. I figured it'd be a while before he could drive, so it seemed
pretty smart at the time.
Whatever.
You know, says Jack, you should do a ceremony for Jervis.
What? I say.
A cer-e-mo-neeee, he says.
I look out the window. Jervis is nattering away in my head. The
truck's kinda like this one, he says. Except bigger. And without all
that rust. Faster too I bet. And the high beams both work.
What ceremony? What are you talking about?
You should go to see that old man. You should ask him about
participating in it. I heard him discussing that ceremony, eh. He
pauses, undoubtedly for effect, then he starts talking real slow
like the old men do. He clears his throat. It was during the time of
the Ground Freezing Moon, just after the new moon, during the
time of...uh...when I...uhm...when I had seen 15 winters. Even
Jack seems temporarily confused by that, and his eyebrows bunch
up on top of his eyes.
We sit there in a stunned silence for a moment, calculating.
Oh brother! I groan. You mean last week?! He ignores me.
That old man, he spoke as the sun moved across Father Sky,
Jack says, and it was then I knew Jervis would like....
I can still see those headlights, Jervis is saying. Ironic, eh?
Oh, yeah, I say interrupting, isn't it ironic! My voice fills the
cab like a hundred arrows flying. Jack stares at me—he knows I
hate it when he does that.

So if you know so much why doesn't Jervis talk to you?! I growl at him.

Jack's hands clench the steering wheel, and he stares straight ahead. His mouth is a straight line.

Yep, says Jervis, it was just like this truck.

My heart starts pounding. Beads of sweat form on my temples. It feels as if a boa constrictor is wrapped around my heart and lungs. Would you quit that! I tell him.

Sorry.

Why can't you just tell me? I ask. It's not like you can't talk. You hardly ever stop! C'mon, I say. Just tell me.

When I wake up I'm standing outside in my pajamas, covered in snow.

A light goes on behind me. C'mon in, says Mom.

We were walking down a dirt road, I tell her.

Yeah, well, do it inside, she says. Where it's warm. She puts her arm around me and guides me into the house. She tucks me into bed like I'm six years old again, and she stands there, looking at me. I look up at her, but I don't know what to say. She turns to leave. My feet are cold, I say.

She walks over to the dresser, opens a drawer, comes back, and hands me a pair of socks my auntie knit. Big thick ones.

She watches me put them on then tucks me in again. Kisses my forehead. When she turns to leave, I clear my throat. She stops and looks at me.

Oh, I say in my deep voice. Sure is cold out, eh?

Yeah, she says.

It's not so much the cold as the dampness, I say.

Want another blanket? she asks.

Sure, I say. In a minute she's back with a big Pendleton blanket, medicine wheel design. She throws it over me and smiles. When she turns to leave I say, Uh...

She stops and looks at me.

Uh, I say. That crazy Jervis.

She picks up something from the dresser and walks over to the window by my bed. When she steps away, my dreamcatcher is hanging there throwing feather shadows across the bed.

Have a good sleep, Son, she says.

I stare out the window for a long time. But why? I keep asking. Why?

———

Maybe it's like that movie, ya know, that one where that kid sees ghosts! says Duck.

Duck always has an answer for everything. Some theory or something. And it always ends up as a warning. That's how he got his name. He almost ended up being called Chicken Little, except that he has that funny voice and that big ole ass that wobbles from side to side when he walks. That's one thing about nicknames around here. Nothing is considered too private, too embarrassing, or too mean to tease you about. It's kinda nice actually, 'cause the names are a sort of acceptance in an Anishnaabe sort of way. Like nothing is too terrible. Got anorexia? You might get called Stick like my cousin Meredith. Real name Lucas and got three fingers burned off when you got drunk and set your house on fire? You're Cool Hand Luke. Even Jack's name isn't really Jack.

Like maybe Jervis wants ya to do something for him! Ya better be careful.

Maybe, I say.

Maybe he's lost, says Jack, and you're the only one who can assist him in finding the way to that path, that path of stars.

Duck and I stare at him. As if he knows anything about that. Jackshit.

Maybe you got special powers for seeing ghosts, says Duck. Like The Old Lady can read dreams, or like I know when the smelts are running, or like Jack can talk to birds.

Jack can't talk to birds, I say, glaring at Jack. Jack just shrugs.

Just as an example, I mean. Like if he could.

Great, I say. I... I see ghosts. I whisper it like that kid in the movie.

AND talk to them, says Jack.

And talk to them. Whoopee. I'd rather be able to predict lottery numbers or know how to disappear when I'm walking in the bush like old Sasquatch.

Yeah, man, that's cool! Remember when we went deer hunting with him, eh, Cuz? You'd look and he'd be like 20 feet behind you, and next thing he's 10 feet ahead, and you didn't see or hear a thing. Spooky!

All of the hunters were able to do that back in the time before the Shaaganaash, says Jack. All of the hunters for our people could walk like that.

We think about that for a while.

After a while Jack says, You could banish him.

Who? says Duck. Jervis?

I can't, I say.

Why?

I dunno. I just can't. Not yet.

Ya better be careful, says Duck. Maybe the way he got killed was for a good reason. Maybe he's trying to lure you somewhere so he can take your head off!

Duck!

Slowly the story gets told.

Jervis had a girlfriend with long dark hair, big brown eyes, and soft smooth lips. He'd go visit her, and they'd walk along the road, holding hands, kicking gravel, and laughing. When she laughed he could feel a partridge beating its wings inside his chest. He'd walk for miles just to see her and miles more just to hear her laugh. The story was like a long road, full of twists and turns, stops and starts. Some of it was well travelled, some dark and desolate. Some was familiar. Some seemed familiar, but before you knew it, you were lost, going around in circles, taken on a long detour.

One day Jervis didn't show up for their walk.

He was angry at his girl, who knows why now, for nothing maybe, who cares, the reason doesn't matter anymore. He was angry, and he decided to go talk to another girl, one he had just met and who didn't have big brown eyes or a laugh that made his heart fly. Just a girl.

His girl waited and waited for him. When he didn't show she started walking, that much we know. I can see her walking that road, her heart dragging behind her like a dying child on a travois. Yet still believing she would meet Jervis along the way. After a while she probably forgot about the child dying behind her and began to worry that Jervis had been hurt. Somewhere along the way, she must have finally realized he wasn't coming. Jervis wasn't coming to see her. Just after that must have been when her brother Vin met her on his way home from work. He felt sad for his sister because she was so sad. Come home, he'd said. But she wouldn't and she cried and pushed him away. She ran down the dusty old road right into his dreams.

He tried to follow but she slipped away.

When it was getting dark and she didn't return home Vin stopped pacing. I'll find her, he told his mom and he took the old truck out and drove the back roads for hours. He went back home thinking she'd be there, even though his heart was sinking into a deep dark snake pit where his stomach used to be.

For a long time they didn't find her body. Just pieces of her clothing and some blood. It was a man not an animal the old tracker told them. A man took her when she was walking.

When she was looking for Jervis.

Jervis was walking the same road when the lights bore down on him. He searched for her, though everyone had warned him to stay away. It had just been a moment of anger. Just an instant of not loving her. But she'd fallen into that moment and disappeared. Jervis walked the same lonesome road looking for her.

Though he was warned.

When the bumper folded around his body and knocked him into the sky Jervis smiled. He had seen her face in the lights, and she was smiling that special smile that was just for him. Jervis could fly.

He knew the boots that stood beside his face as he lay crumpled on the shoulder. He knew it was blame for not loving her that the boots kicked into his ribs. That it was outrage at his thoughtlessness that the pipe drummed into his skull. And the blade in his throat told him not to tell. Never to tell.

And he wouldn't.

Except for one thing. He did love her.

———

Damn, Tony says. He nearly lost his head for her. Damn near cut right off.

That's sick, says Verna.

What? says Tony. Itsa truth, ain't it?

How do you know? I say.

Look, says Tony. He loved her, she loved him. He got blamed for what happened to her. So her brother beats him to death. Out of love for his sister. So she's dead. He's dead. The brother rots in jail. And Jervis is stuck here. End of story.

But what about the man, the one who took her? I say. What about the man?

That night I'm back in the shed with the truck. Then I'm outside staring at the outhouse and the stone.

When I wake up I'm sweating and crying. I knew Jervis had an ugly death. He talked about it all the time. But it took me a while to find out about his girlfriend and her brother and how love and rage and guilt and blaming had gotten so mixed up. I wake up, and I cry for them. For Jervis who made a small but terrible mistake and lost the love of his life. For his girlfriend who probably died in a hateful way at the hands of a man who'd never been caught, and all the while she knew that Jervis hadn't come to her that day, that she would die alone in that very moment Jervis's love was weakest. And for her brother who loved his little sister but let himself go crazy with blame and rage and despair and killed the most precious part of himself. I weep for all of them.

When I finish I go to see my Mishomis.

———

Hey, says Jack. Lookit this! and he points at the television.

I walk over. It's a cop show telling about the case of a serial killer. I can't stand these shows, I say.

Yeah, but this one's different, says Jack. I put some tobacco down for Jervis, like I do sometimes, and when I came in, this show was on.

Jack is so excited, he's talking like a normal person so I stop and look. I can't help but to watch while Jack prattles on.

The guy passed through here, like 50 years ago or something. There's something almost.... I can't put my finger on it, but ya gotta watch, he says.

I sit down. I can't take my eyes off the screen. The hair on my neck is all right angles.

He killed a bunch of women all over the place, says Jack, his words tumbling over each other like rocks in an avalanche. Really sick guy. He was always travelling, a drifter they said. A loner. Then something happened to him, and he found God and became a minister or whatever, right, working with the homeless. So they never caught him till now...

What's his name? I ask.

...he's like 80 years old or something—killed mostly young Native women. Look, he's got blue eyes and they said he had red hair. They say he's part Native, his mom gave him up for adoption when he was like four years old, she was too young or something. It's kind of sad, actually, foster homes, beaten—so he hated...

WHAT'S HIS NAME? I yell.

Geez, what a grouch! says Jack. You oughta go to a sweat or something.

JACK!

Okay, okay. His nickname was Red. Red, uh.... Geez what is his real name? Something weird. He pauses staring at the ceiling. Hmmm....It's, uh... Atticus....

JOHNSTONE! we both say it at the same time. Jack stops watching the TV and his head swivels towards me.

He killed Jervis's girlfriend, I say. Jack's mouth drops open.

But they didn't say....

He did it. He's the one who killed her.

We found out later that Atticus Johnstone had a massive heart attack, practically blew his heart apart. That was the day after that story aired. Died in his sleep.

That's just the way things happen sometimes. There's no real reason. None that you can see or make sense of anyway. Something happens, it causes a ripple, and maybe years later that ripple hits you. Maybe one person does something and his great-great-great-great grandson feels the impact like a punch in the back of the head. Maybe someone who seems to be a total stranger gets knocked sideways. Or maybe it's him, but lifetimes later when he's forgotten that thing he did, and he can't see why this bad stuff is happening to him now. But we never get away with anything even when we get away with it. We've just put it on credit and one day, we'll pay. With interest on all the sorrow and fear that have accumulated.

Mom comes to my room with a cup of hot chocolate and a couple of pieces of her famous cranberry bread. She leans against the doorframe and tilts her head to the side, watching me ripping big bites of bread off and shoving them in my mouth. She grins.

Megwetch, Mom, I say, spitting little bits of bread and cranberry on my shirt. While I pick them off and pop them in my mouth she answers, ehhenh.

Seen Jervis? she asks after watching me eat for a bit.

Nah, I say between bites.

Jervis disappeared the moment I said that it was that man. I could feel it, like a cold wind. A kind of emptiness like when someone's sitting shoulder to shoulder beside you and when they get up and leave there's a cold space where they used to be. I kinda miss him sometimes but I feel happy 'cause I know that he's probably with his girl now.

You been seeing your Mishomis again, eh? Mom says.

Uh-oh, busted. I stop chewing and discreetly sniff my shirt for smoke. Well, as discreetly as I can with her standing right there looking at me.

When you were a baby, I used to wish you could've gotten to know him, she says.

Yeah, I say. That would've been cool. To have known him when he was alive.

Yeah, she says. She reaches over and moves some hair that's hanging in front of my face. But you know him pretty well anyways.

Yeah, I say. There're all different kinds of ways of knowing, I guess. I mean, it's not so much about life or death, I say, it's spirit.

My mom raises her eyebrows and the lights in her eyes dance like jingle dress dancers. She tilts her head to the side and makes a sort of cooing sound when she smiles at me. It makes me blush but I feel like I have a sun shining inside my chest.

Yes, she says, tousling my hair. It's about spirit.

The Blackbird Cage

There is a cage in a sunlit room. A bird sleeps. A songless bird. In a cage covered with cotton.

The cage is round. There is no beginning, no end. This cage is a trap. This cage is a door. A trap door to freedom. Freedom wriggles and spirals and stretches like a child, for that is its nature.

In another room, breath is drawn. In this other room, dreams come fast and easy to those who sleep. The dreams are of rocks and shells, feathers and tongues, skies and wings. They are of the long ago and the yet to come. They are of bones and seeds, icicles and leaves, the Spirit Moon, Heartberry Moon, and a bear standing in the late snows of spring.

The silence will end when the dreamer awakes and the cage is opened.

———————

I was sitting at my desk making plans to visit my sister and her newborn son when the phone rang.

'Hi, Keesic.' There was no lilt in her voice, just a simple statement of acknowledgment.

'What's wrong?' My sister never called me by my full name unless she had something serious to discuss. And since we joked the most when all was well, serious tended not to be good.

'What's wrong?' More frantic now, fear gathering in a lump in the throat.

'Ma said I should call.' She paused briefly. 'Gran had another heart attack.'

There was a long pause, neither of us wanting the words to make our fears true.

'She's dying.'

The trip was a blur. No thoughts, no images are retrievable. Except one. One before the trip began. Except for the moment before leaving when I stood across from Robby, my supervisor. And the image of her face hangs clearly in my mind. A round face, blanching slightly, brown eyes floating, then lips moving. The sound of her voice, struggling to escape from its throat, cracking notes of assent.

Running through the halls of the hospital six hours later. Finding no one. Awash in a strange silence. Dread, unacknowledged, growing inside. Moving down corridors. Finally, my sister's room. And my father sitting by the window reading the newspaper.

I stood staring in his direction and he looked from behind the paper, snapping and folding it in his lap.

'I can't find anyone. I can't find....'

'They're at Aunt Lila's. Mom too.'

'But... Gran?' knowing the answer but refusing to believe it, ignoring what I knew and asking the question with an odd innocence.

'She's gone.' Just that—she's gone—and picking up the paper. Just that and I am left standing, clutched in the steel grip of a monstrous grief, unable to move legs or arms or eyes or mouth. Just standing immobile, tears splashing through gravity like a salty river moving of its own accord down the banks of my face.

'Go look for Darlene. Go look for your sister.' His hands still holding the newspaper.

I moved instinctively, moving across surfaces, between walls, without thinking. As if a wire had become disconnected. I saw but didn't recognize. Doors, walls, signs, elevators, nurses, people carrying flowers and pushing I.V.s down corridors. My feet knew where to walk and somewhere in my brain the signs were deciphered. Somehow I did not slam into walls or walk over people or trip on my own feet. But I could not have named one thing, not one item or one letter. I could not have looked down and thought "foot" or "shoe." I saw and moved on instinct, not understanding.

And there I was at the glass window where the newborns are displayed.

Darlene came walking out the door from the room where the babies are fed. I turned to her, arms hanging as if my hands were weights, and she put her arm around my shoulder and walked me back to her room.

I had seen the latter stages of dying though I'd never witnessed death itself. My Great Aunt Kayla sprang straight up in bed, her mouth opening and closing uncontrollably, eyes wide open but seeing nothing in the room. And I knew I would never see her again.

The experience was poignant and brief and in some unaccountable way natural and life affirming. My father's death was long and numbing. He never trusted doctors, hated hospitals, and refused to take any medications as prescribed. After he started coughing up blood, they found the cancer. Too late. Within two months he was a witness of who he had been. He was in and out of hospital. His hair fell out and eventually he was unable to walk upstairs unassisted. With all the desperation of medical science, they hacked him apart, and we watched him disappear bit by bit.

He spent the days and nights on a borrowed hospital bed in the living room. His temper, which had never been good, became a seesaw of saintliness and rage. Then, after one particularly pain-filled and irksome evening, he suffered a stroke and one side of his face slipped loose. After that he refused to look at himself in a mirror. Saliva gathered and dripped from the left side of his mouth and his words were limp and slid together into a series of grunts and groans. He rarely slept. When he did, he dreamed of birds clawing their way out of his chest and he'd wake up screaming and moaning. In fits of frustration and anger, he began hurling anything within reach at anyone within range. That stopped soon enough though, when the pain worsened and we had to give him morphine to keep him from screaming night and day.

When he died I was in town buying groceries. When I returned, Darlene, Aunt Lila, and Mom were seated around his bed. Mom was holding his hand and an air of peaceful calm suffused the place. And I felt, I knew without asking, that the pain and suffering had ended for everyone in the room.

Dad's eyes had been closed and, laying there surrounded by family, he looked relaxed and strangely healthy. I realized then how the pain had stretched a mask of disease across his face and now that it was lifted how terrible and solemn it had been. His spirit had attained freedom and in that freedom had shaken loose the body. Without the spirit the body ceased struggling. Without struggle the mask came unhinged and disappeared. As I stood touching my mother's shoulder it occurred to me that the illness had been overcome after all: he was free at last.

———

Gerry is the only man I've ever loved.

We met at a dinner at his parents' home one early spring evening. His mother had become a fast friend after coming to my aid at a poetry reading. Two Greedy Minds had been circling, quizzing me about life on the reserve, Native spirituality, the appropriation of Native stories, land claims, the rights of sports fishermen versus Native fishing rights.... I tried, politely at first, to extricate myself. Then I exuded an intense disinterest that bordered on deafness.

I openly daydreamed. Imagined myself becoming birdwoman, darting and circling to freedom.

To no avail. One persistent, brighteyed university student continued asking about sweat lodges and potlatches while regaling me with stories of her various brushes with spirituality. All with the kind of open faced wonder that could drive a pacifist to throw punches. She stared, hanging on my every word and gesture. My hand was a clenched fist.

Barking in my other ear like a dog chasing his own tail, was a plain, 50-something man with a greying beard and balding head. Like all the worst ones he started out chatting about this and that

"Indian" friend of his before launching a tirade about tax breaks and gun-wielding warriors.

Caught between the two, I was about to step back and knock their heads together, *very hard*, when a woman grabbed me by the elbow, saying very sweetly as she hurried me towards the door, 'we'd like to say it's been a pleasure... but it hasn't.'

We left, politely nodding and smiling right and left.

Outside, we walked without talking. The air was as cold as knives in our lungs and we slowed, pulling our scarves over our mouths. At the streetlight, she turned to me. 'I'm Joan. Hi.'

'Hi.'

'Tough room.'

'No worse than most, I guess.'

'Scary thought!' We laughed together and I knew then that we would be friends.

Gerry came to the dinner late, with a young, slightly drunk woman hanging on his arm. He grinned and shook my hand warmly, saying a line from one of my poems as he did so. It made me laugh and we chatted amicably for a few minutes before the meal was served. Shortly afterward he and his friend shouted their goodbyes from the foyer and left, laughing and slamming the door behind.

I bumped into him several times during my visit, always sharing a smile and small talk. A kind of friendly disinterest characterized all of these meetings.

———

When I was a child of seven or eight, I found a blackbird injured at the foot of the glass doors of Gran's sleeping cabin. And I borrowed Grannie's old birdcage and placed the bird inside. Within a few hours the bird was sitting up, looking around curiously. But I was afraid he hadn't fully recovered. I was afraid to release him in the dark, on such a cool night. Instead, I put a margarine dish of water and some sunflower seeds inside and covered the cage with a piece of white cotton. Then I went to bed happily, dreaming about how Bird would sing in the morning. And when he was completely healed, I would release him. He would circle around my head in thankfulness, he would dip and dive in his unfettered joy at being saved. And though he was free, Bird would stay with me from then on. He would sit on my bedroom windowsill chattering secrets in birdtalk.

Early the next morning, as sun streamed through the window, I anxiously lifted the cotton. Bird's dead eyes stared up at me from the bottom of the shining chrome cage.

———

Gerry has eyes the colour of a late winter afternoon sky. A deep vibrant blue-black, warm and penetrating. My German father had blue eyes but they were implacable, like pools of cold water. And he could hide his emotion easily beneath their cool surface. Gerry's eyes are filled with shadows and valleys, fierce storms and gentle rain, midnight skies and the soft hues of dawn. When I look into their changing colours it is as if I can see everything he is thinking and feeling. And the first time I kissed him it was his eyes that had drawn me in.

And from that moment, I fell into him with abandon.

———

A room, pale yellow and shining. Rows of sunlight through slats reflect on chrome. There is a disturbing lack of depth. Everything is flat, white, bright, antiseptic.

There is another room within the room. A place where dreams have space. A place for real living.

Whispers leak around the pale yellow room. Hissing, shifting, shuffling. Bodies under bright white cotton. There is no screaming that can be heard.

Our coming together was like glancing up and seeing a sky filled with falling stars. In a dark room with the tea kettle bubbling, we touched unexpectedly, accidently almost. And there was a moment when our eyes widened. As if to say, who are we? Who is this 'we' that two people become, who this 'us?' And I looked into his eyes and I kissed him full on the mouth, swallowing his words. Then tongues meeting, probing, loving, a new language was born. A language like all language and unlike any other, unlike any we had ever known. Tongues pressed against teeth, lips against lips, creating the sound of this language, the lilt and pattern of it, the glottals and sibilance. Together, with the kettle steaming and shouting behind us, we became the grammar and expression of this language. And through us punctuation and diction arose. A lexicon was created. And spirit pervaded the language.

Gerry gave me gifts collected on the beach down the road from his mother's home. Every night I would find a shell, a stone, a feather on my pillow and every morning I would awaken with new eyes, new ears, and a full heart. So it was that meaning was conveyed and understood and gained depth.

And his mother was a quiet observer to what we were becoming. Without intention, she became the ears to our mouths and tongues, the listener who realized the sound. Without her, it is possible we might have slipped into another world, the world of dreams and spirits, and forgotten our way back to the threshold. We might have slipped and never found life in this world of earth and sky. This world where babies suckle their mothers' breasts and the forest hums the energy between trees. This world of our waking existence.

A screaming bird battering itself against gleaming bars. A blackbird crying in a cage of bloody, hacked off beaks.

I am sitting in the living room of our home. Gerry enters, cold and sweating. Before I can speak he collapses at my feet.

Since then I have seen his eyes, through a mask of pain, struggling to give expression to this thing. To find words for what cannot yet be understood. Since then I have held him through long nights in strange, cold rooms. And held his head, stroking his sweat-slicked hair, as he retched and shivered.

Sitting on plastic chairs, I have waited. I have waited. I have listened to the odd echo of heels clicking on tile, my ankles absorbing the coldness. I have seen images of bone. Images of heart and breath and stone. I have watched an image of heart and breath, rising and falling, rising and falling. The heartbeat an unsettling beep and silence, beep and silence. I have surrendered my dreams to a thin green line.

Between visits to this cold, bright place, we lived happily. But as this thing grew and Gerry weakened, a terror intensified. And the between folded back on itself. Then the cold place became home and home, the visiting place.

There is a figure of a man. A silhouette on snow. Snow and sun and a solitary man stumbling.

31

Snow blindness. Eyes burn and water. Blinding whiteness. Snow and sun and a solitary man stumbling.

The barrens. No beginning, no end in sight. A circle of white. Snow and sun and a solitary man stumbling.

———

I could not bear to look into Gerry's eyes then. Could not bear it in the yellow room where more and more days and nights were spent. Could not bear it in the living room. Could not bear it in the bedroom. For the first time, I began to close my eyes when we kissed. And a silence rooted itself in our tongue.

So, for a time, a space grew and it was you and I, he and I again. And a new mask was fashioned for each. Gerry's mask was a thin transparency that exposed and highlighted his eyes and mouth. Mine covered my eyes and ears. This is how we might have continued in freezing, quiet desperation.

Then one day, Gerry fell on the hard, white tile, knocking the masks loose. And in that instant I saw a blackbird standing in the corner of his eye.

———

There is a child waiting to be born. And Gerry and I weep together, our hands encircling my already swollen belly. We have remembered our reason for being and the tears are a language all their own. Translation is inept.

When our tears have said all that can be said, I whisper to Gerry in the language we have come to speak fluently. His eyes are a beautiful oratory of understanding. Now, again, Joan is our ears. Now, she has become paper upon which our words are written.

As prayers are recited, family gathers. So the ceremony begins and ends and continues in a circle of language.

I open the cage door.

The Stone Eater

BEFORE DAWN, SHE WOULD RISE. HER MOCCASINED FEET shuffling through that old house, its lights off, floorboards worn smooth. In her room, she would pull on a thin, loosely fitting slip, a flowered cotton housedress and a sweater before going into the bathroom to scrub her face, hands and teeth. She would scrunch up her face, stretching and yawning, thinking of the grandchildren laughing and running and yelling for her to make funny faces for them. Then she'd strain her old eyes into the mirror hoping to catch a glimpse of the young woman she once was, before popping her teeth into her mouth.

Later, she would cook porridge and make toast and tea. She would eat at her small chrome table looking out at the bay. When she finished, she would carry her bowl, spoons and "Pow Wow 1983" mug to the kitchen sink. She'd wash the dishes, rinse them in scalding hot water, wipe the crumbs from the table, and put everything away. Afterwards, she would clean fish, slicing their bellies open, chopping off their heads, scaling them and scooping out their red-brown guts, tossing them into a bucket for the cats. Or maybe she'd sew moccasins. Or make scone. Sometimes, she'd make quilts or she'd go into the bush to gather plants for teas and medicines. Most days she ate fish and greens, potatoes, and scone for dinner, sitting at her place in front of the big, bay window.

By the time supper rolled around she would be tiring. Not when she was younger. But once her body began stooping closer and closer to the earth, as if she was getting ready for one last embrace. Her supper these days was good and fast. Soup and salad. Not like when she cooked for her old man and the kids. When the food was piled on the plates. They worked hard then. All of them, together. And ate heartily. Needed to and were thankful. Didn't waste, took what was needed and left the rest. Always did.

After her evening meal she would listen to the radio or watch television. She liked watching game shows. Said the greed was fascinating, 'like watching dogs fight,' she'd say. Except "Wheel of Greed" as she called it. She didn't like that one at all. "Using the circle like that," she'd say wrinkling her nose. "Sah."

She was no prisoner to greed. Kept her doors and windows unlocked day and night, year after year.

"Haven't got anything to take," she'd say. "If someone needs what I have so badly they can come in and get it. Must need it pretty bad. No point being locked up in my own house. No point having someone bust a door or window to get in."

After school, children would drop by to visit. "Ahnee, Nokomis," they'd sing out.

"Umbeh," she'd say. "Umbeh. Nahmahdbin," jutting her lips at the kitchen chairs. Then she'd make tea or hot chocolate and feed them fry bread and jam. Sometimes those kids would help her sew moccasins or haul water or stack wood, chatting and laughing the whole time. They would tell her about their lessons and their teachers and wait for her stories. She'd tell them that one about Nanabush and the chickadees or about Nanabush and the Indian agent. Sometimes she'd tell them about their own families. Map out who was related and how, where so-and-so was buried, or about men who drowned while out in their fishing boats, or babies saved by various herbal treatments, or about buildings that burned in fires and who was inside and died or who should've been inside and escaped certain death.

Some days those kids, they'd come to her crying. Crying because some white kids called them "wagon burners," or because their teacher said something shitty about Indians in front of them.

"Aupitehih igoh nawh w'gageebawdizih!' she'd say.

Or they'd come in crying because they just found out that not having a status card meant they weren't considered part of the land that had always been their home.

She'd hug them. 'Ah, neen binogeehns, you know who you are," she'd say, repeating their names over and over, tracing their ancestry. "That's what matters. We're all relations you know. We got that blood, that same blood. Remember that. And remember the land don't belong to anybody. We belong to her.' Then she'd give them tea and pat their hands. "This land, she knows you. She isn't gonna forget you," she'd say. "Remember. Remember and you'll always know who you are."

The children would believe her too. They'd stop crying and drink tea with her, asking more about the web of family relations, about the land, about the history that led them to her kitchen table that day. Before leaving they'd be laughing and telling funny stories about one another. Then they'd split and stack some wood for her and carry buckets of water into the house from the pump.

That way she'd be ready for the next morning, they'd tell her, and they'd smile, putting their hands over their mouths or sticking their skinny chests out and swaggering around the yard with their knees pointing sideways like their dads and uncles. Yeah, those kids would believe her and they'd leave feeling good about themselves and their place in the world.

After her visitors left and before she went to sleep she'd brush her long grey hair. One hundred strokes. She'd tie it with ribbon, like a bundle. Then she'd pull back that worn pink bedspread, and, while she was staring out the window at the stars, she'd give thanks for the day. Slowly, she'd rise, turn out the light and as she settled into her bed and fell asleep she'd talk to her husband, C.K., who she believed was waiting to take her to that other world.

But all that would come later.

First, each morning, on a table by the back door, she kept a small bundle wrapped in cotton and tied with ribbon. Before dawn she would open the back door, breathing in the moist cool air. She'd go out, the bundle held tightly in her left hand. She'd walk down the sloping backyard, and that early morning dew would coat her soles and rub against her shins. At the shore she'd stand on the stones waiting for the sun to rise from the water.

That night, that particular night, in the early morning darkness, those guys got into the house easily through its unlocked doors. She must have heard the noise and slowly, in that quiet way of hers, stepped from the bathroom into the triangle they formed. No words were spoken. Then, as the blows pounded, the fists and hammer and cane cracked into bone, thumped into her soft flesh, there were no screams. Not one cry for help. Just a gulp of air, a gasp as her chest was slammed with fist or wood.

Then that voice, quiet and respectful in the throes of such pain.

"...Kitche Manitou..."

My hair stood on end.

I ran to the kitchen. That old fish knife with the broken wooden handle was there by the stove. I ran with it. Saw six arms rising and slamming into her. I ran with the knife. Raised my arm. Slammed it into her neck. They stopped hitting her then. She fell to the floor. Blood spurted, she fell and they stopped hitting her. They stopped hitting her, howled and went swarming through the house grabbing the few things she had, smashing what they didn't want or couldn't understand. I lifted her into my arms and stumbled through the back door.

Outside I turned four times then placed her on the stones. I pulled the knife out quickly and the stones turned a deep sticky red.

As the sun rose I picked up blood-stained pebbles and stones, placed them in my mouth and swallowed.

Forgive. Forgive. Forgive. Forgive...

That is how they found us in the early morning sunlight.

Now they ask me over and over again, *Why? Why? Why?* But how do you explain a moment when your world is turned inside out? Some say I ran with the devil; some say I became a hollow spirit, a pauguk. They may be right. I was like a dog running with a pack. Hoping it would keep my enemies at bay. How do I tell them I set those dogs on her trail?

Some say that what I did was satanic but they are wrong. That I drank her blood. That I am insane. But they are wrong.

But why? they ask. *Why? why?*
I am here waiting for the answer too.

So I tell them that she was wearing that white cotton sweater I had given her for Christmas only months earlier. "For something special," she said, holding it to her chest. I tell them how we laughed together and how I felt a kind of happiness as we peeled oranges and ate in silence.

I could tell them about nights of drinking, about needles and smoke and a haze of sex, drugs, and fighting that made me forget everything except an emptiness I couldn't escape. I could tell them about shaking and sweating, puking until my throat was raw. I could tell them about other break-ins. Other blood. Other bones cracking. I could tell them about living without feeling any ground underfoot, about being non-status, non-knowing, non-feeling, non- remembering.

But instead I tell them how she would rise in the still-dark morning.

The Palace

SHIT.
Saturday night and I'm broke again. Not that there's anything much to do here on a Saturday night. Except it's not just any Saturday night. It's New Year's fucken Eve. Jackie-O, Mukwa, DJ-D, and Aces are making a booze run soon 'cause we're all heading to The Party Palace later to ring in the New Year. And I don't have any coin so I can get myself a six-pack or even some of that cheap fizzy wine girls like.

I wander down the hall and peek into my little bro's room. He's 10 and full of piss and vinegar. He dresses in secondhand clothes because he wants to and he always looks good even in stupid looking shirts from a decade ago or jeans that are too tight or too baggy to be cool. The kid's got style.

"Jims?"

He's building a city out of Legos. Doesn't look up. "Hey, buddy?"

Still doesn't look up. "What?" He's digging in his pile of grey Lego. He's got all of his Lego neatly sorted into colour piles. Red. Black. White. Yellow. Grey.

"Whatcha doin' tonight, bud?"

"Dunno. Goin' to Noko's with Nim and Rave. Mom and Dad are partying at Uncle Tommy's, so I'll prob'ly stay at Noko's."

"Get spoiled, eh bro?"

"Guess so."

Nokomis will have a bunch of snacks for them, maybe a few videos she rented for 'em, nice clean beds. She and Pops'll stay up till midnight. She'll give the kids those noisemaker things you blow in and twirl around. And they'll toast in the New Year with cranberry juice and soda water. She'll hug and kiss everyone. Pops will make a little speech about this year being the best one ever then he and Noko will head off to bed, leaving Jims and the other grandkids to stay up in front of the TV, gorging on chips and candy, drinking pop, and goofing around until the sugar buzz wears off and they all crash in front of the TV, or crawl into their beds. Noko will check on them later, put the ones on the floor into bed, make sure they're all covered up and tucked in, and kiss them goodnight.

"Cool."

I'm still leaning in his doorway. He looks at up at me.

"What?"

"Whaddaya mean 'what?'?"

"Whaddaya want?"

"Shit, dude. Can't a guy talk to his little bro on New Year's Eve without him gettin' all suspect?"

"Sure," he says, still eyeballing me.

"Just wanted to make sure you were okay for tonight."

"Uh-huh." Hasn't taken his eyes off me.

I stand there with my hands jammed in my pocket. I can see at least eight bucks on his dresser beside a Batman Band-Aid, some twist ties, a jackknife, a pack of apple Warheads, a scrunched-up newspaper article about Dudley George, and a tobacco tie. Above it is a poster of a fiercely beautiful Native Hawaiian activist and one of her poems. *I wonder where he gets this stuff*

"Wanna play Lego with me for a little while then?" he asks, the little bugger. "I mean since it *is* the last day this year that we can spend time together and all." He grins at me all innocent like.

The little shithead has me on that one and he knows it. His eyes are twinkling at me like they're full of little stars.

"Sure!" I say, as if it's the best idea I've ever heard. As if all along I was just dying for him to ask. I go over and sit on the floor. Flick the hair outta my eyes. Pick at the red and green carpeting that's older than both of us put together. Then I choose a couple of pieces of red Lego and stare at them.

"I'm building Washington, DC," he tells me. "But like all bombed out and destroyed. And the White House is gonna be all wrecked and everything. And there's gonna be all these flowers and trees and animals inside. Like there's gonna be an orangutan living in the Oval Office 'cause the animals at the zoo all got out too, eh. And it's like the trees and everything are taking it all back. Starting over 'cause Bush and them made such a mess of things. And anyway, an animal'd do a better job than him anyhow."

Wow. Jims is a fucken smart kid. I dunno how a 10-year-old comes up with these crazy ideas. He's always reading. Always trying to save the planet and all that shit. "Cool, Jims. Very cool."

I snap the two red Legos together.

"So, uh, I was thinking of going out with Jackie-O and them tonight." I don't tell him that Mukwa and Tiny and that posse are gonna be there. Jims hates it when I hang out with them.

He doesn't say anything. He takes the red Legos from my hand and sticks them on a building.

"But I haven't got any money..."

He stops what he's doing.

"...you know, like for snacks or so I can have a toast at New Year's with everyone."

He gets up and digs around in his dresser. Then he comes over and hands me a $10 bill. It's from his birthday money. If I didn't feel lame already now I feel like a total shit.

"This enough?" he asks.

"Yeah, man. But I can't take this, dude. It's your birthday money."

He shrugs. "Take it."

"But..."

"Take it. Just don't get in trouble, okay? With Tiny and them. Okay?"

"Okay, Jims."

"Promise?"

"Sure, Jimbo. It's cool. I just wanna have a good time. Start the year off right. With my friends."

"Some of your friends are assholes."

"Jimmy! You shouldn't talk like that, dude."

"Well, they are."

"They're our cousins."

He can't argue with that. Blood is blood. He sits down. Pats his ponytail. Scrunches his eyebrows together.

"Don't worry." I muss up his hair. He squirms and reties his ponytail.

I stand up. "Hey, have fun at Noko's, eh. Don't get all strung out on sugar and do something *crazeee*." I grin at him.

He looks up and flashes me a smile. Little brat has something planned, I can tell. Last year it was a water balloon fight in the rec room. Noko made him carry wood for a week for that one. Although when he wasn't in the room she laughed her head off about it. The brats hit Pops right in the back of the head with one and kept running. He was so surprised his eyes nearly popped out and he spit tea all over his lap and down his pant legs.

"Damn kids!" he roared, staring at the spilled tea that looked suspiciously like a pee stain spreading across his crotch.

"You kids get back here." Noko was trying to sound stern but couldn't help smiling. Pops jumped up and rubbed his hands together then took after them. The kids screamed, Noko laughed, and Pops, grinning like a crazy man and looking like he'd just wet himself, went flying around the corner at full tilt.

Fuck, I wish I'd been there to see that.

The dogs pace, bark, and howl when Jackie-O, Mukwa, DJ-D, and Aces pull in front of the house in DJ's shitty old rust-bucket 4Runner. Fucken guy spent three times as much on the stereo, which is blaring Pink Floyd, as he did on his truck.

"It's just transportation for my sound system, dude."

"Yeah, great. When I'm sprouting wings and heading to heaven after the brakes give out I'll be so friggen pleased by the audio clarity of the GNR song wafting up from the wreckage."

"Hey, shut up!"

"Yeah, I'll be like, well, yeah, okay, I'm dead because D's rez-mobile was such a shitbox it fell apart and killed us, but man, the bass sounds awesome on *Paradise City*."

"As if a dickwad like you'd be getting into heaven anyways."

"Yeah, Jelly, you've committed all the deadly sins."

"And that was just last weekend!"

They all laugh at me.

"Laugh all ya want. I'm a fucken saint and you know it."

"Well, ya got that right. That's the only kinda saint you'll ever be."

"Well, if you're good, you're good, eh! What can I say?" I puff out my chest.

Jackie-O hits my shoulder. "Yeah, you wish."

The guys laugh and hit their thighs. "Shot down!" they howl. Jackie-O and I have gone out a few times over the past couple of years. One of those on again/off again things.

D is just givin' 'er all the way into town. We get there in like 10 minutes. Run into the beer store, grab a 2-4, and get the hell outta there. We divvy it up at the back of the truck. We each get six 'cause Mukwa wants to head to the LCBO for rye instead. The rest of us put our six beers in plastic grocery bags and line them up in the back. We throw a ratty old blanket over them so they won't roll around. Mukwa runs into the liquor store and gets a 40 of rye.

"Holy shit, man," says Aces. "Planning to get off yer face or what?"

"Fucken hope so," he says. "Tiny and I are splittin' it."

Jackie-O and I raise our eyebrows at each other. This can't be good. Not fucken good at all.

D turns off his lights when we get close to The Palace. We all crane our necks to look at the house. The front porch light is blue.

"Party!" Mukwa yells.

Four heads swivel in unison.

"Shhhhhh!" we all say moving our arms up and down in that turn-it-down-dude way.

"Yeah," growls Jackie-O. "Shut the fuck up!"

Mukwa hangs his head and is silent.

Man, that J-O is one tuff chick. A shiver runs up my spine. Damn, I miss that girl.

Blue light means the party is on. It's still early though—so early hardly anyone is there and the music is still at an acceptable level. We decide to go have a few at the gravel pit before heading in. By then it should be insane.

We do a bunch of dumb shit at the gravel pit to pass the time. D and Aces argue over which of the identical bags of beers is whose and roll around in the snow for a while.

"What are ya? Ten years old?" Jackie says with an edge of disgust in her voice that could shrivel a man's dick in milliseconds.

They stop wrestling and look at each other.

"What are ya? Ten years old?" they say together in weirdly high voices. They laugh, high five, then go back to rolling around in the snow.

Meanwhile, Mukwa is having a moral dilemma about his rye. He knows that if he drinks it without Tiny he'll possibly get the shit kicked outta him. But if he doesn't we'll tease the shit outta him and he'll be the only sober one when we get to the party. Either way he's in shit.

"Grow some balls, man," D says. "D'ya think that if Tiny was here instead of you he'd spend one second worrying about you? Drink your damn rye."

"I was going to," Mukwa says.

"When?" I say. "What are ya waitin' for?"

We all stare at him. He cracks under the pressure, just as we knew he would, twists off the top, and takes a long haul just to prove he's no wuss. But by then no one gives a damn. Aces and DJ are in some weird competition for J's attention. Now they're having a spitting contest. Jackie and I lean against the front bumper, watching. It's really stupid.

But it *is* kinda cool that Aces can spit through his front teeth.

Aces wins for both distance and style and takes several bows.

J rolls her eyes. D runs up behind, gets Aces in a headlock, rips off his toque, and gives him a noogie. Aces doesn't look so cool standing there rubbing his head.

"Jackie," I say, taking advantage of the fact that I'm the only one actually sitting with her. "What's your resolution?"

"To get away from these assholes," she says nodding her head towards Aces and D who are now having a pissing contest. An actual pissing contest. No shit!

Mukwa turns up the tunes.

"Axl Rose," he says. "Now, there's an asshole."

I jump off the hood of the truck.

"And here's another one!" I yell before launching into an awesome air guitar version of *Welcome to the Jungle*. After all, a guy's gotta compete.

We shut off the truck, turn off the lights, and coast in behind some cedars just down the road from The Palace. We always park here so we can get in and out easily. It's also good if one of us snags and needs a place to...ya know, get in and out easily. Plus, even though it's shit on wheels, D is always worried about someone breaking a window or puking in the back seat or something. Fair enough. Things can get totally outta control at these parties.

We stroll into the yard like we've been there for hours. Jackie slips in with Pechi, Stick, Sally, Roxy, and a group of girls hanging by the fire. D punches Junior Odemein in the arm and clinks his beer into Junior's protein shake or whatever the hell he's drinking. Aces goes and stands by the fire. Man, he must have it bad for Jackie-O tonight. Meanwhile, she's totally ignoring him. Mukwa is looking this way and that with his eyes as big as a friggen bush baby's, as that rude bastard from American Idol might say. He's sheepishly taking sips from the 40 pounder. I see Tiny go stomping towards him.

Better run interference. I step in front of him.

"Hey, bro, how's it hanging?" I throw my arm over Tiny's massive shoulder and pretend to be more drunk than I am.

"Good, man," he says his eyes still firmly on Mukwa who has finally noticed and is making his way towards us.

"Cool," I say, swaying a little—finally, 10th grade theatre arts class is really paying off. "Mukwa's been looking for you all night, dude."

I can feel Tiny's muscles unclench.

Mukwa stops just to the right of me—and just out of arm's reach to Tiny.

"Let's have a toast!" I yell. "Woohoo."

Mukwa hands Tiny the bottle then steps back out of arm's reach again. Tiny wipes off the mouth with his sleeve. I smash my bottle into his, and we both guzzle.

"Happy New Year!" I yell again, for dramatic effect. Damn! I am *really* good at this acting shit.

"Yeah!" Tiny yells, getting into the spirit of it. He takes another drink and hands the bottle back to Mukwa who takes a granny sip.

"Gimme that bottle," Tiny says to me. I gulp the last mouthful and hand it to him.

He pours rye into it and hands it to Mukwa. Mukwa looks like a kid who has just dodged a beating. Which he has.

Mission accomplished. I fake stumble away, grinning a dazzling grin that lights up the sky and melts hearts for 500 square miles. Hah! Take that Adam Beach. *Dude.*

*And the Oscar goes to...JELLY J! *thunderous applause**

I'm living my dream, I say clutching the gold statue of the naked neutered guy. *And even though I've spent my career giving Hollywood the finger... You like me.* I say. *You REALLY like me!*

Just then Betty the Bomb saunters past.

"Wuh," she says and rolls her eyes. "Get a life."

I know she wants me.

"My people will call your people, babe!" I say, pointing my index fingers at her and pursing my lips Zoolander-like.

Adam who?

Over by the fire, Cole is strumming on his guitar. He's got the blues. The lowdown Anishnaabe blues. Lorene K. strolls over. Now that girl can sing. She listens for a few minutes then she's off.

Got the blues, neechee...

"Oh yeah," we yell.

Got them ain't-had-no-bannock-in-a-long-time blues...

"Eh-henh!"

I said I got the blues, baby. Got them no-bannock-in-a-long-time blues...

"Tell us!" Duck calls out

Well, you take a piece of dough and you roll it to and fro

Then you take it in your hand and you put it in your pan

'Cause you know I like it hot and you know I like it slow

Yes, I said I like it hot, I like every bit you've got

We laugh. John-john wolf whistles.

But tonight I got the blues

Got them no-bannock-in-a-long-time blues

How do I like it?

"Hot!" we yell.

Yes, I really like it hot, I like every bit you've got

But tonight I got the blues

Got them can't-get- me-no-bannock-in-a-long-time blues...

Lorene's buzgim Reuben yells out, "Don't panic girl, I've got you a big piece of bannock!"

We all crack up. Lorene throws her beaded buckskin glove at him but keeps singing.

I don't want some little crumb or bannock smaller than my

thumb... She wags her thumb at him. We all laugh and hoot and holler. And keep on singing.

A few minutes before midnight all the couples are looking for each other and the rest of us are jostling to find someone kissable to stand beside. At midnight we yell and clink our bottles together and kiss the cutest person around us. DJ and Aces set off some firecrackers.

After that, the music gets progressively louder. Voices get louder. The drinking gets louder. Everyone is trying to score something. Drugs, more booze, or a snag.

I talk to Lorene and Reuben for a while. They're leaving before things get crazy.

"I just wanted to hang with the cuzzies on New Year's for a bit," Lorene says. "Have a couple of beers and toast the new year."

"Yeah," says Reuben. "The baby's over at Dad's. I just want to go chill out with her and Lorene for a while."

Sounds like a good way to start the year, I tell them. Although I can do without the baby thing for a few years. But I don't tell them that.

After they leave I wander around looking for D and Aces. They're always pulling some prank and having a good time. I can't see them by the fire so I shoot the shit with Jack, Winona, and Fizz for a while then head towards the house.

Inside, people are arguing or making up. Some are just trying to stay warm. Couples are sneaking into the bedrooms, closets, and dark corners. So many people are staggering and wavering on their feet that I feel like I stepped onto a boat or train. A few people have passed out. Beneath them the floor is wet with tracked in snow and spilled beer. A heavy cloud of smoke is hanging above everyone's heads. The stereo is blaring Breach of Trust at eardrum-breaking levels.

There's a tension in the air, like just before the big storm hits. I drift back outside. When something happens, and it usually does, I don't want to be trapped in the house. I look for Jackie-O. I wanna make sure that when the shit comes down she'll be out of harm's way.

Outside I see that Tiny and Mukwa have polished off the 40 and are now drinking someone's beer. They're totally off their faces and acting like pricks. Tiny throws his empty beer bottle into the fire, sending sparks flying.

"Hey!" someone yells.

He spins around and swaggers towards the fire with his shoulders back, ready to wage war.

Jackie-O pipes up from across the fire. "Hey. You're spraying embers everywhere."

Tiny glares at everyone then lets his shoulders droop when he looks at Jackie. "Sorry, Jacks."

She glares at him. "Watch it, eh? This is my new jacket. *Geeeezz.*"

He turns back to Mukwa and strides off with his back real straight and his arms flexed. He sure is one big mutha-fukka.

Everyone breathes a sigh of relief. Jackie's the only one who dares talk to him like that. Her mom took Tiny in when he was a kid and his dad was drinking and beating on his mom. Noko said it was probably the only time in his life Tiny felt safe. He was a bully and troublemaker everywhere else but around Jackie's house he was golden. Jackie would put ribbons in his hair and get him to have tea parties with her. And he would! Us little kids would play hide-and-seek and Tiny would pick up Jackie and run with her. Guess who always won? Yep. Whatever Jackie wanted, Tiny did. Still does.

Anyway, now I know where she is. I walk over. Stand beside her with my thumbs in my pockets. She looks at me and nods her head.

"Hey," I say. She nods at me. "Colder'n hell, eh?"

"Yeah."

"Party's starting to turn," I say jamming my hands in my jeans pockets and standing tall.

We look around. Someone's puking in the bushes. DJ and Aces are pantsing the drunk guys who are still standing. Reuben's ex, Lulu, is bawling like she does at every party around this time. A few guys are arguing about something that doesn't make any sense to anyone else.

"Were you inside?"

"Yeah. It's worse."

"I was gonna head out soon anyways."

"I'll walk ya."

"Okay," Jackie says. "But I wanna say goodbye to Tiny first so he doesn't worry."

We take a couple of steps away from the fire. A pair of headlights turn in the driveway. Right away we know it's not one of us. But who? The cops probably. We're all ready to run. We hold our breath and wait. Then we hear guys arguing and a girl screams. Everyone at the fire runs towards the driveway.

"That's Tiny," says Jackie. "Hear him?"

"Yeah. He sounds pissed."

Jackie takes off running. I run after her.

Tiny and some guy are screaming at each other in front of an old Lincoln. Mukwa and the guy's two buddies are glaring at each other.

"What the hell's going on?" I ask Duck.

"Oh, it's really bad," he says. "We better get outta here before someone gets killed."

Typical Duck response. I turn to Fizz.

"I dunno, man. I think that's the guy who ran over Bobcat last year."

"But Bobcat was drunk and stepped in front of his car."

"Tiny said 'dead is dead' and took a swing at him."

"Not necessarily," Cole mutters.

"But anyways, aren't they from The Lake?" I say. "Those guys are our cousins."

"No one is even sure he was really the one driving," Fizz says.

"I heard he took the blame to protect his girlfriend," Cole says.

Cole always seems to know what's really going on before the rest of us.

Jackie yells for Tiny to stop. "Go home," she tells the other guys. "Get the hell outta here."

There's a moment of stillness. Then Tiny lunges at the guy. The poor guy manages to get off one or two punches before Tiny takes him down. His friends try to pull Tiny off. Mukwa jumps on them. While those three are thrashing around Tiny sits on the guy's chest. His fist is a sledgehammer. A young woman cries out, "Wigawaykee!" and takes a run at Tiny. Her friend grabs her arm and struggles to hold her back. Just then Jackie runs forward. She's screaming, "Stop it! Tiny! Stop!"

The guy is barely moving now.

Jackie grabs Tiny's arm. He swats her away and she goes flying. He's never done that before. Ever. Now we're really scared.

I run over to help Jackie up. "I gotta get you outta here," I tell her.

"*Kawee!*" she yells, pushing me away and running back to Tiny. He pulls his massive arm back to throw another punch. She wraps her arms around his arm and digs her heels into the snow. Tiny is furious. She keeps repeating something in his ear. He hesitates just long enough for a bunch of us jump on him and pull him off the guy. He bellows and fights all of us but we manage to hold him down. Aces and D tackle Mukwa and pin him to the ground.

"Get outta here!" I hear Jackie yelling to the guy's friends. They run over and pick him up. He's like a rag doll. They shove him in the back seat. The girls they brought with them are sobbing when they jump in with him. The car speeds off. Us guys look at each other, nod our heads, *one, two, three,* and then at the same time we all jump off Tiny. He sits up like King Kong bursting free of his chains. He looks this way and that, ready to pulverize anything that moves. After a few seconds, he relaxes slightly. We stare at him. His knuckles are scraped and he has some other guy's blood splattered all over his jacket. Then he sees Jackie. He falls back and lays there, chest heaving, running his hand through his hair.

Jackie is sitting in the snow, crying. I sit beside her. Jackie throws her arms around me. I hold her and help her to stand.

A small group is milling around the spot where Tiny was beating on the guy. Even from here I can see the blood flowers seeping into the snow. There's a thick, sweet smell in the air that makes me want to gag.

DJ, Aces, and I drive Jackie home. We all stare out the windows. Cedars, leafless maples, and pastel-coloured houses roll in and out of frame, like images on a movie screen that flicker for a moment, then are gone. When we get to her place, I walk Jackie up the lane way to her front door. I give her a hug. For just a moment, she rests her head against my shoulder and exhales slowly.

The house is dark when I get home. I close the door as quietly as I can, tiptoe to my room, and sink into the bed. I feel like a stone, sinking into sand.

When I wake up the next day, my mouth is dry and sticky like I've eaten paste. I open one eye. Jims is standing there staring at me.

"You okay?"

"Yeah." I wonder how much he knows? I stare back at him.

"Tiny and Mukwa got arrested. That guy's in a coma—he almost died."

"Shit," I say.

"Assholes," he says. "I know, I know—cousins. But assholes."

That damn kid is always right.

"Well, I'm glad you're okay," he says. We stare at each other for a few moments. "I hear Jackie is okay too..."

I raise my eyebrow. Now what?

"... since you took *such* good care of her." He winks and backs out the bedroom door. "Wooo, woo..." he calls. Nothing gets by the little brat.

I throw back the covers and sit up ready to give chase when all of a sudden, it hits me.

A water balloon. Right in the crotch.

Jims covers his mouth and laughs then goes tearing out the door and down the hall.

I jump up.

Holy hell my head hurts.

"You better run," I yell.

"*Ooooh*," he calls back. "*Quiver*! I'm *sooo* scared." Then he laughs and I hear his footsteps as he runs through the kitchen.

I can't help but smile. *Little bugger.* I run out into the hall. After taking care of Jims, I'll give Jackie a call.

Calcified Horses

MY TEETH ARE LITTERING THE SIDEWALK IN FRONT OF MY NOSE. They're the first things I see when I come to. I can't remember if I broke them when my face hit the concrete or if it happened before I plummeted to the earth like a US spaceship. All I know is it's a horrible feeling waking up with pieces of yourself strewn about you.

I stay stretched out like that breathing through the pain. My gums are bleeding and my jaw hurts like hell. The sidewalk is ice. I raise my head but it only lifts a few centimetres. The teeth still left in my head are chattering. Spikes of pain stab straight into my skull until I pass out again.

Someone steps over me. Then another person. *Friggen drunks!* I hear a young man's voice say. A woman laughs. *Les indiens!*

Drunk? *Drunk!? Screw you!* I try to yell out to them but I can't seem to move my jaw. How did I get here? I can't remember falling. "Please," I hear a familiar voice saying. "She needs to go to the hospital." It's my cousin Fritzy. My body is a giant net of pain. My guts and hips are on fire. My head is throbbing. It's as if a herd of wild horses stampeded across my torso then rose up on their hind legs before slamming their front hooves into my head.

"Fwwshheee," I call out. My voice is a thin reed, wavering on the small breath I can send through the holes in my now-clenched teeth. I groan.

People are arguing. I float in and out of this world. I see herds of palominos racing across badlands, the shifting shadows of storm clouds moving over their outstretched necks and legs. Hear waves of sound: *"drunk" "hit crossing" "squaw" "move her" "needs help"*. Most of the voices are angry. A few are whispers spit at me as people walk past. I hear a flock of geese, wake, and realize they are cars with horns honking. I see geese flying. Some of them fall from the sky and land with a splatter around my body as if making a chalk outline with their blood.

When I come to again, I'm on my back with my head in Fritzy's lap. Her face is a contortion. I see outrage, fear, and a world of grief I've never seen in her face before. It scares me. I want to comfort her. I feel a tear roll down my face. "It's okay now," she says. "It's gonna be okay. We just need to move you, okay?" I blink my eyes.

I don't remember getting up. I must've passed out.

The walk to the car is excruciating. Two women are helping us. Fritzy and one of the women have me under each arm and are half carrying, half dragging me towards a dark sedan. It's cold. So cold. I feel like concrete setting. Snowflakes land on my eyelashes, melt and run down my face like tears I can't wipe away. Another woman is running ahead. The one helping me walk says she's a nurse. "Everything's gonna be okay," she tells me in that soothing voice nurses use. "We're taking you to the Civic Hospital." When they lay me down on the leather of the back seat she looks at my eyes and holds my wrist. Her face is tight, as if a stocking is pulled over her head. I can see the veins in her temple bulging when she leans over me. Her face is soft but there's a slow simmering in her eyes. What's happening? My thoughts are a scrambled TV signal. I see Fritzy stepping out of a cab and remember sliding across the seat and stepping onto the snow-covered street. It's New Year's Eve.

I see snow falling and a snow-covered street.
Fritzy laughing.

The nurse's lips are moving but they're out of focus and float around her face.

At dinner Fritzy and I had laughed about the New Year's Eve when we were teenagers on the rez and each had two dates. We ran back and forth between two parties where the two sets of guys were waiting to ring in the New Year with us. We tried to cover for each other, made up elaborate stories, pretended the other was in the bathroom or kitchen or outside smoking when really she was at another party altogether. I see our New Year's party dresses flying as we sprint from one house to another, shoes in hand, running in bulky winter boots through slush and mud. By the end of the night, however, we'd both been caught, not only by our two sets of dates, who all immediately dumped us, but by everyone at both parties.

"The shame!" we cried, laughing. But it was the most fun New Year's Eve either of us had ever had and we've talked about it every New Year's Eve since. I smile a crooked broken-toothed smile at the memory. Even slight movement shoots arrows of pain into my skull. Tears roll down the sides of my face. I know they're mine because they're warm and leave little trails of salt on my face before being absorbed by Fritzy's coat.

Streetlights roll past the window. I know we're in Ottawa now but I'm not sure where. The lights blur and merge. We careen around a corner. I hear a tight "Sorry" from the front. But we don't slow down. I'm dizzy. I keep trying to hold myself down. Hold myself in place. Tell myself exactly where I am as if each detail is a nail hammering me to this place. *I'm on my back in the back seat of a stranger's car. She's a nurse. Leather seats. Dark sedan. My head on Fritzy's lap.* Fritzy's resting her elbow on the window with her wrist bent and her hand in front of her mouth. Her other hand is stroking my hair. So delicately. She thinks I'll break. Everything is slipping in and out of focus. I cling to the pain because I know it's real. And I know now something terrible has happened. Fritzy's my cousin. We grew up together, like sisters, on the rez. I can read her face even through my swollen eyes and near-blinding pain.

My heart starts racing. Suddenly through the pain, another feeling reaches up and grabs me by the throat. For an instant, I'm terrified. I want to sit up, open the car door, and run screaming down the street.

No. No! It's not supposed to be like this.

It's not fair. Tears roll down my face, hot and blinding. *Haven't danced at my wedding with the love of my life yet. Haven't had a baby or gone skinny-dipping at midnight or camped in winter under a canopy of stars. Haven't been given flowers and choco-lates on Valentine's Day from a man whose eyes twinkle when I walk into the room.* Blurry faces appear and disappear in front of me. The boy I loved in high school. Friends from the daycare

60

program where I worked every summer while I was at Algonquin College. *Wish I'd had a baby.* My nieces and nephews. *Married that young man who seemed "too boring" all those years ago.* His face disappears. I see my parents in their garden, bending to the earth. The faces of all of the men I loved and let go fade in and out of sight. If only I could tell them what they meant to me. If only I could make it all right with each of them. *I'm sorry. It was beautiful, so beautiful.*

Then Fritzy's face above me blurs and bends, wavering in and out of focus. I see her lips move and seconds later, from far far away, I hear her voice like a distorted echo travelling across mountains and fields.

I close my eyes. *Live a good life.*

The spikes in my head are twisting and turning like iron snakes. Horses run across my skull. Their hooves pound into my brain. I hear a drum beating. The horses dance across my head in rhythm to the sound of the drum. My teeth are rattling. There is a lake of blood in my head, filling my throat.

There is the sound of water rising.

"No! Josie, no. Hold on." Fritzy lifts my head, staring at me, then pulling me to her chest. She yells to the women in the front. Their voices are stones hitting together underwater. "Josie," I hear Fritzy whisper desperately in my ear, "please."

A rattlesnake sighs.

I can barely hold on. Feel myself floating. The pain that had grounded me now sets me adrift. Streetlights fade then fill the car until all I can see is a single white light. Voices fade into the rhythm of drum and hoof beat.

The horses stomp their feet.

Mashkii-akii

WHEN JUSTIN ROOT HIT THE GROUND, HIS LEGS CRUMPLED
sending him face first into the dirt. A fraction of a second later, the
branch, which was still tied to the rope around his neck, smacked
him in the back of the head, knocking him senseless.

When he woke, his heart was thumping in his chest like a jack-
hammer. He groaned. His friggin' nose felt like it was on fire. Was
it bleeding? He struggled to breathe. His ribs ached.

Awww, damn!

Justin didn't move. He stayed sprawled against the earth, breathing
in dust and the smell of his own blood, until his pulse slowed and
the clouds in his head cleared.

After a while, he moved his right arm forward and wiped his hand lightly across his nose. *Yep, blood.* When he tried to breathe he could feel bubbles forming in his nostrils. *Damn.* He spit and tried to wipe the dirt from his teeth and lips. It was gritty and he'd already swallowed some. His Nokomis always said that everyone eats a pound of dirt in a lifetime. She probably didn't mean for him to do most of it in one go. Or that the span of his lifetime would only be 14 years for that matter.

He shifted position slightly. And groaned again. He was one big pile of ache.

Justin exhaled through clenched teeth until his breathing slowed again. *Anyway, what difference did it make?* He would just stay there until his body melted into the earth. When the buzzards, worms, and creepy-crawlies were finished, that'd be it. End of story.

The sun was directly overhead now. It must be lunch time. Justin could feel beads of sweat gathering at his temples and above his upper lip. The armpits of his shirt were soaked. He was glad he wasn't wearing shorts and a t-shirt—he'd be fried. The skin where his hair was parted was burning. Good thing he wasn't wearing sandals. Burned feet were the worst. There was a large rope burn on his neck and every drop of sweat that ran over it stung like a thousand hornets.

Not that it mattered. What did he care? He was trying to get rid of this stupid meat suit anyway.

If not for the stupid branch snapping he'd be free of it and floating above himself like a cloud right now. He closed his eyes and imagined floating.

When he woke again, hours had passed. The sun was edging closer to the horizon. Blood had dried around his nose and across the left side of his face where it had run over his cheek and pooled. He opened his mouth wide and moved his jaw back and forth. His headache was gone and his nose had changed from a raging wildfire to a small glowing ember. His ribs sent stabbing pains into his chest and back, his ankles were probably sprained, his knees were scraped and bruised, and it all rolled together into one big throbbing ball of pain. He was used to that ball. It matched the one aching in his chest. The one that, like a *windigo*, grew bigger and bigger the more he fed it. He pulled the rope over his head then slowly—ever so slowly—he turned over. These bodily aches and pains are insignificant, *like flies buzzing around my head*, he told himself.

The sun was setting. The ground was still warm and, somehow, comforting. He would stay like this till sunrise. Then he'd find a sturdier branch and tomorrow he'd do what he'd set out to do at sunrise this morning. He stretched out on his back watching the sky turn from blue to gold to pink to grey to black.

His guts were churning. He ignored it just as he ignored the pain his fall had caused. *It's only temporary*, he told himself. *It's not like I've never gone to sleep hungry. Or battered, bruised, and nauseated. Why should tonight be any different?*

It became an obsidian night, glinting and sparkling. From his spot on the escarpment it seemed as if Justin could reach up and touch each star in the sky above him. He watched the constellations shimmer and pulse. He thought about the stories his Noko had told him about women and men who fell so deeply in love with stars they would transform into Star People to join their lovers in the sky.

No one has ever loved me that much, he thought.

As he lay there, staring at the Seven Sisters, he heard a small voice.

"Have *you*?" it asked.

Had he what? He was angry, daring the voice to speak again.

There was no response. Justin lay there thinking about the stars, about Noko, about tree limbs at sunrise, and about his life with all of its agony, heartache, and disappointments. Why had his mother brought that asshole into their house?

He was only six years old when Mike showed up one night for dinner. The idiot was all dressed up in a freshly pressed shirt and jeans. *That should've told her right then. Who the hell irons their jeans anyway?* When Justin opened the door Mike was standing there in his unwrinkled jeans, holding a bouquet of red carnations, and grinning like the cat that swallowed the canary. *Puke.*

Mike grinned all through dinner. The only time he stopped was to shovel food in his face. He even grinned when he chewed.

After dinner he made a big show of helping with dishes and giving Justin a little pocket knife. Mom didn't want him to have it, but Mike insisted.

"What? D'ya want him to be a sissy?" Then he smiled again.

It was the first time Mike said that. Over the next few months the firsts came fast and furious: the first time he screamed, the first time he pushed, the first time he hit…and there was always that sneering look at mom and those same old words.

The relentless smiles turned into a permanent sneer after Mike moved in that summer.

Didn't Mom see the bruises? Didn't she notice how he'd walk a Frankenstein walk so he could keep his mangled body as still as possible? Didn't she hear him groan when a sudden movement sent shock waves of pain shooting from his jaw into his brain like nails of lightning were being hammered into his head? If Justin was even the tiniest bit a sissy, Mike made it his personal mission to beat every last ounce of it out of him.

The stars moved closer. *Damn. I was just a kid. A little boy. Why didn't she stop him?*

Mike lost his job shortly after moving in. Or rather it lost him. He just quit showing up. He'd go sit in a bar or at some greasy spoon instead. Or he'd lie on the couch all day, eating Cheetos and beef jerky and swearing at the "losers" on *Maury* and *Judge Judy* with their pathetic problems that were "their own damn fault." After that he never worked. But he'd eat a big thick steak Justin's mom paid for while they ate macaroni and ketchup. If Justin so much as looked at the steak, Mike would slam down his knife and fork, grab Justin by the collar, and throw him into his room for the rest of the night.

Justin began dreaming about food. Steaks and sausages, stacks of pancakes dripping with maple syrup…. Sometimes the rumbling in his gut was so bad he'd steal food from other kids' lunches at school. And he'd eat whatever he could find. Once, when he was seven, he ate green apples until he couldn't eat another one. He spent the rest of the night doubled over in the outhouse. After that he learned to be patient enough to wait until things ripened and to eat until the hunger left and save the rest. He tried to convince himself that the emptiness in his stomach was good, that it made him strong.

Justin felt a knot in his chest tighten. *Life sucks.* Why did they live there anyway? So far from everyone, never enough to eat, no one to help them.... Why? And the other kids blamed him for every-thing. Money missing, broken windows, graffiti on the school, crank calls—you name it, if it happened in his neighbourhood and it looked like a kid did it, Justin was blamed. Until the day a group of kids came by his house and knocked all the blooms off of all his mom's flowers. When Mike came storming out they pointed at Justin.

"You little bastard," Mike bellowed.

"They did it." Justin waved his arm towards the group of kids shuf-fling their feet by the sidewalk. The other kids called him a liar.

"No way. Justin did it," one of the girls said.

"Yeah," the others chimed in, "Justin."

Liars!

"But...I was trying to make them stop." He knew what was coming and began edging away from Mike's reach.

"Next time, try harder!" and with that Mike took a step forward and backhanded Justin across the face sending him reeling back-wards. Justin could hear a couple of the girls gasp. They weren't accusing him now.

"We did it," they were saying. But Mike wouldn't stop. Mike never stopped. Justin could hear the girls crying. Somehow, it made him feel better. They *should* cry. They deserved to cry for what they did. *Bullies. Assholes.*

"But I didn't even do any...." Mike punched him in the side of the head. An image of two of the girls clinging to each other, their eyes wide, like doors thrown open, was the last thing Justin remem-bered before he blacked out.

He had a pounding headache when he woke. But he never got blamed by the kids at school for anything *ever* again. Even when he did do it.

It was a relief. It was almost worth the beating—that one saved him a hundred other ones. A few of the kids were even nice to him now, though he wasn't sure if it was compassion or pity that drove them to it. Anyway, Mike still found reasons to beat on him. He left the cap off the toothpaste or he walked too loudly or there was a "tone" in his voice or he was "grinning like an idiot" or he didn't "look happy enough." If Mike couldn't find a reason he invented one.

Justin stared at the night sky. The land seemed to soften beneath him, and he let himself sink into it.

"Stand up straight, my boy," Mishom would say when he and his mom would visit Mishom and Noko at the rez. Justin walked slouched over and hunched in on himself. A habit formed from years of protecting his stomach and ribs from sudden punches and kicks. A way to make himself small and unnoticeable.

Justin shifted position on the ground. Some of it was a long time ago, but his body remembered everything.

He searched the sky for the Seven Sisters. Could he find them? He tried to imagine falling in love with one of them. As he watched them, the stars moved closer. They moved closer and closer until he could feel them dancing in his hair.

Had I? he thought, staring at the shimmering lights. He tried to think of people in his life whom he loved—really loved. He thought about his mom. Disappointment filled his lungs. He exhaled slowly. He'd been angry with her for so long now. Blaming. Resentful. His dad was only a vague shadowy figure standing in the doorway, barely remembered. Justin was only two when his dad drowned in the stormy waters out by Rabbit Island—what he felt for him was abstract and idealized. Justin had a couple of friends and there'd been a couple of girlfriends too. He liked them. But he never brought them into his world. They never saw his room. They never saw the scars or bruises. They never heard about his dreams, not even the small ones. Not any of them.

He couldn't get the thought out of his mind....

Have I? he thought. Over and over again. *Have I ever loved anyone as much as those men and women loved those stars?*

He saw Nokomis and Mishomis waving from the front porch whenever he and Mom left to go back to the city. He'd kneel on

70

the back seat and wave until long after he couldn't see them any-more. He'd try to memorize how they stood, the expressions on their faces, the way the sun or moon lit their hair and fell across their hands as they waved. He studied the trees and rocks and clouds until even the gravel and stones at the end of the driveway faded from sight.

Justin felt a summer storm gathering in his chest. Noko and Mishomis never let him down. Except for one thing. They left him. They didn't mean to, he knew that. If they could've they would've stayed with him. They would've stayed forever just for him. But still, they were gone. He was alone.

Then, for the first time since he was a little boy, Justin Root cried. After the accident that took them away, Justin was too numb and too scared to cry—especially with Mike watching him constantly, telling him real men didn't cry and to "suck it up like a man." To "quit acting like a snotty nosed kid." To "stop moping around." To "get over it." But here, held by the earth, Justin cried. He cried with great heaving tear-filled sobs that made his ribs and heart and throat throb with a pain much deeper than that caused by his recent fall. He rolled onto his side, pressing his palm into the ground. His body shuddered and shook. Justin cried until all of the tears he'd held inside soaked into the dirt around his body. He cried until he slipped into a deep, technicolour sleep. And when he did, the earth and roots beneath him formed arms, cradling him as he dreamed.

———

When he woke, the sun was overhead. It was well past sunrise. Justin stretched and yawned loudly, scratching his belly and rub-bing his fist into his eyes.

Then, slowly, he stretched again.

He sat up. Looked from side to side.

He breathed in and out. Then he breathed more deeply. He lightly touched his fingertips to each of his ribs. His neck. Felt the back of his head. Wiggled his ankles and toes.

He jumped up. Ran on the spot. Leaned down and touched his toes. Nothing.

With all of the subtlety of a hurricane, he realized he was as hungry. "Hungry as a horse." Mishom would say. And had to piss like one too.

Eggs, he thought dreamily. *Pancakes, venison sausages...*

It was strange how good he felt. Two days ago he'd walked and hitched all the way back to the rez so that the last thing he'd see would be this piece of sky and the last thing he'd feel would be this piece of earth. Now here he was—ready to sprint to the nearest kitchen. He had a cousin, Velma, who had a couple of little kids. She was always telling him to come to her place. "Come and stay," she'd say, smiling a megawatt smile that would make him feel like he'd just been hugged. It was like somehow she knew. Probably Noko and Mishom had told her to watch out for him. He laughed and shook his head. From the corner of his eye, he saw it. A rust-stained patch of earth. He touched his nose.

Justin remembered being a very small boy in the bush up on the escarpment with Noko and Mishomis. Everything had the golden glow of late summer. They'd seen a similar patch of earth and

Mishomis told him that when animals are injured they will lay their wounds against the earth. "For healing," he said.

"She's the best healer," Noko said. "When you're hurt, come lay your wounds against the earth."

Justin kneeled down. He had no tobacco. So he sang a song, the most beautiful song he could sing. Shaky and tentative, newly formed, and slightly off key. Then he leaned forward and kissed the ground. "Megwetch," he said. He looked up to the sky, "chi megwetch." He saw the broken tree branch and the birch rising above it, stretching itself toward the sun. "Megwetch," he said. The branch's weakness had saved him. He wouldn't forget.

Justin knew it would take a long time to fully heal. That some of the wounds he had were hidden in dark places, locked up, thrown into deep wells within him. He knew he'd have to let go of his mom, that he couldn't protect her any more than she had been able to protect him. He knew he had to build a new life for himself, here where Noko and Mishom were close and he could learn to walk tall and straight again. He knew what he had to do.

He jumped to his feet and raced down the path before him.

Eggs, he thought as he ran towards Velma's. *Pancakes and venison sausages....*

Mirrors

.

"AW, JEEZUS!"

Thomas Kendasswin looks at the long hair, the slender wrist, veins pulsing timidly under the hint of skin, and he wants to throw up. His lips pull down at the edges and curl. He sees her body move slightly with each breath. He watches, thinking how he wants to plant his feet firmly in her pale, narrow back and push her out of his bed, out of his room, out of his house. Out of his memory.

"Shit!"

He sits up slowly. The mattress barely moves, and the headboard and springs that had rattled and squeaked in the dark are hushed and silent under the glare of morning light. He sits on the edge of the bed, holding his breath, listening for changes in her breathing, for movement. Good. He rises slowly, shifting his weight carefully. Last night's boxer shorts are at his feet. He kicks them with his toe then plants his right foot on them and stands there heavily. Go without he decides before spying a clean pair on his dresser. Hah, being disorganized has its benefits. On his way out of the room he lifts a pair of almost-clean track pants from one of the piles of clothes on the floor.

He stops at the top of the stairs. The television is on downstairs. Damn, shit, damn! He grabs a t-shirt from the hamper in the bathroom, sticking his nose in the armpits. Deodorant. Cologne. Faint smell of sweat. Okay, good enough. He washes quietly then brushes his teeth and combs his hair. He shaves the patches of whiskers on his face. Next, he applies a slap of aftershave, coating of deodorant, spray of cologne. Finally, he slips back into his boxers, t-shirt and track pants. Ready. He opens the bathroom door and sticks his head out, listening.

When he gets two thirds of the way down the stairs, Thomas starts walking normally, pounding his feet on the steps and swinging his arms. He even hums a little for good measure. As he passes the living room on the way to the kitchen he calls out as cheerfully, as sincerely, as he can muster.

"Good morning!"

"Morning, Daddy."

"G'morning."

He breathes deeply, opens the fridge and takes a long, gulping drink from the jug of orange juice. Thank christ he remembered to have her park her car behind the shed. Now he only has to figure out a way to get the kids out of the house quickly, without waking her up or arousing their suspicions.

Thomas leans the back of his head on the fridge and exhales a long, deep breath. He hangs his head and stares at the floor in front of his feet. Seeing his children makes him feel like he does when he goes into the bathroom and comes face to face with himself after a night of smoking and drinking himself into a stupor. He's seen that image of himself too many times lately.

But he doesn't want them to see it.

He hides that face from them. Muffles the aching emptiness in his chest. Sneaks strange women into the house in the middle of the night. Sneaks them into his bed. Women with whom he could never laugh. Women who look at his skin and hair and boots and think he is someone else. Women he could not talk to or sing songs about or cook for.

Standing in the kitchen, Thomas has a sudden impulse to move the bathroom mirror, angle it so it reflects the sky. He wants the mirror to reflect the tops of the maple trees. He wants the mirror to reflect the hawks and hummingbirds, blue jays, cardinals, and eagles. He wants the mirror to reflect the storm clouds and lightning, rainbows, and leaves blowing in the wind. He wants the mirror to reflect the rain, snow, sleet, and hail. He wants the mirror to reflect the sun and the moon and the northern lights. He wants the mirror to reflect the colours of a Saugeen dusk and dawn.

But the mirror is fixed to the wall.

Tomorrow, he thinks, leaning his shoulder against the fridge. Yeah. Tomorrow he will remove that mirror and replace it with a better one.

Thomas strides into the living room. Great, the kids are dressed.

"Hey, guys," he says, grinning. "I don't wanna cook. Who wants to go out for breakfast?"

"Me. Me. I wanna go." Raven is smiling and moving her right arm around like she's in school and desperately needs permission to leave the room.

"I dunno," Nim sniffs, still staring at the television. "I already had some cereal..."

Oh, you little weasel. Thomas stares at his son. Without glaring. Sweetly. Patiently.

"...Where we gonna go?"

"Well, where do you want to go, Nim?" More grinning.

"Maybe if we went into town," the boy says in a monotone. "Maybe if we went to *Stacks*, I wouldn't mind getting some pancakes." He acts about as enthusiastic as a death row inmate.

"Yeah, great idea, Nim," Thomas says with just the right degree of interest reflected in his voice. Yeah, just great. *Stacks*. In the mall. Beside the toy store. Across from the arcade. Great. Thomas tries not to roll his eyes at the same time that he tries not to sound like the phony that he is. "Sounds good, eh Raven?" She makes noises of agreement and bobs her head up and down with all of the eagerness that her older brother lacks.

Thomas moves around, turning off the TV, wiggling and jamming his feet into already-tied Nikes. "Okay, let's go or by the time we get there it'll be too late to get breakfast."

"Daddy, should I take my sweater?"

It's probably upstairs. "No!" That sounded too desperate. He tries again. "Uh, no, I don't think you'll need it, Sweetie. I think your jacket's in the hall closet. I'll grab that, okay?"

"All right, Daddy."

Nim is halfway up the stairs before Thomas notices.

"NIM!"

Turning, eyes wide, his face a question mark. "What?"

"Oh. Uh, what're ya doing, buddy?" Another fake smile. He could run for prime minister at this rate. Or Grand Chief.

"Getting my Gameboy." He sticks his lips out. "Jeez."

"Son, we're in a hurry," waving him back downstairs. Nim doesn't move. He looks towards the top of the stairs then towards his sister. Then back towards the top of the stairs. Thomas grits his teeth. He smiles like he imagines Sir Francis Bond Head smiled at his ancestors at treaty time. "I thought, if we have time, we'd play a game at the arcade."

"Cool!" Nim bounds down the steps about as quietly as a herd of buffalo stampeding across plywood.

Thomas's shoulders hunch reflexively and he has to force himself straight. Then, while attempting to look as though he's not listening, he listens intently for any responding sounds from upstairs. Still nothing. So far, so good.

He gathers their jackets from the hall closet, ties Raven's shoes, hands Nim his Grizzlies cap, and sticks a pair of Oakleys on himself to hide his eyes. Then he ushers the children out the front door, pulling it closed behind him. He doesn't bother to lock it. Never does. He is breathing normally as he walks to the truck. The children are running and laughing in the still-cool morning air. Like colts they kick up their legs, run a few steps and toss their heads. They run to him, give him a nuzzle, chase each other across the overgrown grass and rocky outcroppings of their front yard. Thomas smiles watching them. He stands straighter and his chest expands and tightens at the same time. He leans his arm against the hood of the truck and stands watching his children. His children. His children with their long black manes of hair and gleaming teeth. With their teasing and their laughter always bubbling beneath the surface. With their bright, black eyes, clear, shining, and bold. His children who are so much like him, they remind him that there was a time in his life when he was truly happy. When he could face anyone's gaze without flinching. His children who are so much like their mother that he wants to laugh and cry and hold them close to him and never let anything bad happen to them.

"Hey," he calls. "Umbeh." He nods his chin towards the truck. "C'mon, Nim. Rave."

He opens their door and they scramble into the back seat as if they are all angles. He helps Raven with her seatbelt, kissing the tip of her nose to make her laugh. Meanwhile Nim has put his seatbelt on by himself. He sits there with the kind of careful nonchalance that reminds Thomas of the way the Chief sat at the Community Centre moments after being re-elected. Thomas nods at his son. "Good," he says with enough husky seriousness in his voice not to patronize. The boy nods and tries not to appear pleased although his eyes shine and his spine straightens slightly.

Thomas subdues the urge to hug him. To hug them both.

The sun glints on the windshield and chrome as Thomas walks around the front of the 4x4. Truck could use a bit of a wash, he thinks to himself. Someone should open a car wash here on the edge of the rez. Good summer business with these dusty roads. He opens the door and slides into the driver's seat. Better wash the truck while we're in town. The kids like that. He turns the key in the ignition, pulls his seatbelt across his lap and chest and buckles it. He checks his mirrors and reaches for the stick shift. Oh yeah, better pick up that bathroom mirror too.

"Hey, Nim."

"What?"

"Remind me to get a new bathroom mirror when we're in town, okay?"

"Why? What's wrong with the old one?"

Thomas' brow wrinkles. "Nothing." He shifts in his seat. "I just wanna get a better one." He swats at a horsefly. "Just remind me, okay?"

"Yeah." Nim stares out the window. "Whatever."

"Daddy, will a better mirror make us look better?" Raven's voice is serious and thoughtful. "Maybe we could get one that would make me big like Nim."

"Raaaven!" Nim snorts and laughs. "Mirrors aren't magic. They just show how you are."

While Nim is speaking Thomas steals one last furtive look at his bedroom window. No sign of movement. Good. He can feel the mask sliding from his face, can feel his real face shifting and reshaping itself as he shifts the truck into reverse. In a moment he'll be home free. He breathes deeply, letting his shoulders droop slightly.

"Hey, Daddy?" says Raven.

"Ehn-heh?" Thomas smiles, glancing in his rear-view mirror at the back seat.

"Aren't we gonna wait?"

"Wait?" Thomas' head pulls back slightly and he looks intently at the faces of his children in the rear-view mirror. "What for?"

"For that lady."

"That lady sleeping in your room."

Thomas stares in the mirror as he backs down the driveway.

Butterflies Are Free

WHEN FREDA LIFTED HER SON FROM HIS HIGH CHAIR, CALLED the dog, slung the diaper bag and her purse over her shoulder, grabbed her keys and, on impulse, the family photos on the hall table, and walked out the door she had no idea where they were going or for how long. She only knew that her son's laughter was all the wealth she needed, and she would go wherever they needed to be to keep it safe. She didn't actually think of it that way in that moment on that morning. Something inside simply propelled her to the other side of the door, down the creaking wooden steps, into their new club cab Ford Ranger, down the gravel driveway, past Mishomis's old place, and west past the boundary line, past the borders of the rez, past the surrounding towns, down roads she'd never driven, far from every place and everyone she'd ever known.

As the telephone poles slid past the truck windows, she counted her blessings: her son, their health, a bit of cash, some skills and talents, and a family and community that would remember and accept them when they returned whether it was next week or on her long journey back to the earth and stars. The sun moved closer to the horizon and they stopped for gas, nearly on empty, at a place she didn't recognize. She pushed her long dark hair out of her eyes and leaned into the back of the seat. The sun slanted between the maples, birch, and cedars, landing on her chest like a giant laser. Her chest opened wide exposing her heart. Her pulse raced but she felt a strange sense of calm move over and through her like a current. She opened the door and got out to pump the gas. The air was cool and fresh, a potent mix that combined memories of melting mid-winter snow-storms with the promise of warm summer days spent lounging on sandy beaches.

She filled the tank and paid with her debit card at the pump. She got back into the truck, rubbing her hands together and grinning at her son in the rear-view mirror. She would need to start paying with cash, she realized.

"Juish?" her son said. He smiled. He was always smiling.

"Juice," she said. She unbuckled him from the car seat and took him inside the little store. It wasn't getting dark yet; she guessed from the angle of the sun that it was only about 2 p.m. She bought juice, milk, water, bread, peanut butter, jam, cheese slices, and a large green tea. She paid for it with money from the beaded wallet her baby's Nokomis had given her, then asked the gawky-looking teenaged clerk where the nearest First National Bank was. Next town over, he figured. Right at the next lights about 25 minutes or so, left onto Main Street. Like, ya couldn't miss it, eh. Big square red-brick building, big white columns in front.

The kid was polite enough though he looked through them, barely acknowledging their existence. But that was better than the balding old man behind the counter, probably the owner, whose steely grey eyes brazenly stared at her turquoise jewelry and her son's long hair and stone turtle necklace. When she'd asked the kid about the bank the old guy's eyes narrowed. Did he think she was heading over there to rob the place? That she was a scout about to join her band of wild Indians as they set off to attack the money train in some old western? His lips curled slightly and on her way out she felt his eyes on her back, measuring her height as she walked past the chart stuck to the side of the door.

"Five feet five," she called out as she stepped outside.

She sat Negik back in his car seat, gave him a sippy cup of watered-down juice and half a cheese sandwich. He grinned. "Thakoo, Mama!"

She leaned against her door and watched him eat, plucking out the cheese first then picking at the bread like a sparrow. Sun streamed in the window against her back. She sipped her tea and melted into the seat.

When Negik finished his sandwich, he dropped the crusts which were promptly gulped down by the dog at his feet.

"Buster!" she said. Buster looked guilty—but not so guilty that he would stop sniffing for crumbs. Certainly not so guilty that he wouldn't do it again. Buster was a small, goofy looking rez mutt. Except that no dogs are mutts these days. They're 'Golden Doodles,' 'Chorkies,' 'Affenpoos,' 'Spoodles,' 'Jugs,' 'Chugs,' and, as she liked to call them, 'Shih-T-Poos.' Buster, she liked to say, was a Dogle: part Miniature Doberman, part Beagle. He had the coat and markings of a Doberman along with the slender legs and pointed muzzle. Unfortunately, he also had the big, floppy ears and clumsy feet of a beagle as well as the loud, baying howl. He was not a pretty dog. He was fearless but lazy, had a great nose for dropped food and garbage, and was a good watchdog— if one can convince oneself that a dog barking at strangers from the comfort of his bed or from his favourite spot under the couch is a good watchdog. Nevertheless, Negik loved Buster and what Negik loved, Freda loved too.

She fastened her seatbelt and drove to the bank. She emptied her bank account and then emptied their joint bank account too. It was mostly her money anyway, and there was no doubt that he'd live in her house until every bit of food was gone, the hydro and cable were disconnected, he had found and spent her emergency cash taped to the bottom of Negik's diaper pail, and he'd taken everything he could haul out of the house and sheds. And what he couldn't haul away, he'd throw out or destroy unless her cousins showed up to put him out. She pictured them, arms crossed in front of their barrel chests telling him to go, pointing for him to put down whatever he was carrying, then putting their hands out for his set of keys. Jake was a big guy, former high school wrestling champ, but he'd obey them. People were scared of their quiet, nothing-to-lose, never-back-down persistence.

Outside the sun was moving closer to the horizon. Freda silently counted the small Ontario towns they drove through. She tried not to think about what she'd left behind. The sweater that had belonged to Mishomis. The nightgown her granny had made. The books of poetry she'd stood in line to get signed. Auntie's rag rug. Flowers from her sister's funeral that she'd dried and kept in the top drawer of her dresser. Negik's baby book. With its ink footprints, lock of baby hair, and first scribbles.

Buster whined and pawed at the floor. At the next side road, she pulled over, put his leash on him and walked him around the car. Before putting him back at Negik's feet, she scratched behind his ears and told him he was a good little nimosh. She stood and watched her son who was drawing on her cheque book with large toddler-sized crayons. "Are you okay, my boy?"

"Fun, Mama," he said. He giggled, scribbled another wobbly looking spirally shaped being, and pulled her closer. "Fun."

She leaned down, sniffed his hair, then breathed out slowly.

the day I learned to fly

THE DAY DAWNED AS CLEAR AND BRIGHT AS A SQUIRREL'S EYES. Which are pretty damn clear and bright by the way. Although I don't know about those red squirrels—a red squirrel is about as jittery as a crack addict. Not that I've ever seen one. A crack addict I mean. I've seen lots of red squirrels. Anyway, it was a great morning. As that Carpenter chick might've crooned," not a cloud in the sky, got the sun in my eye." The songbirds whistling in the cedars, the aroma of coffee hanging in the air like a spell, Jesse with his bed-head hair, wearing nothing but boxers, fixing breakfast over an open fire. Ahhh...what more does a girl need?

I took a few minutes to curl up in my sleeping bag and ease into the day. It reminded me of those summer mornings of my childhood when I would wake in the little back bedroom at my grandparents' house on the rez. I'd stay in bed enjoying the smell of breakfast cooking and the warmth and peacefulness that permeated the house. I could sometimes hear chickadees or the chatter of chipmunks. Soon I'd be drawn out of bed by the promise of food and my curiosity about the laughter and conversation in the kitchen. When I'd wander into the kitchen still wearing my pajamas, rubbing my eyes, and yawning, my grandfather would tease me. "Dawn of the living dead" he'd call out. "Here's one of the zombies now." Everyone would laugh. Usually, that was my cue to walk with my arms straight out, legs stiff, eyes staring straight ahead until I reached the table and could swipe a piece of bacon. (Back when I still indulged in the pork.)

Outside the tent, Jesse was humming. I smiled and stretched but didn't rise. I'd never been with a man who made me feel as safe and happy as I felt those summer mornings at my grandparents' home. Until that moment.

"You awake?" Jesse called to me.

I stretched.

"Or do I have to come over there and get you up..."

"You'll have to come and get me," I teased as I stretched out, waiting.

When I was a child my grandmother told me stories about an old woman she knew as a child. This woman was a Bear Walker and my grandmother, although young, had heard stories about her for as long as she could remember. The woman's granddaughter, Elsie, was my grandma's childhood friend. One time my grandmother stayed at this girl's house overnight.

"We slept upstairs in a loft with her grandma. During the night, I woke. Moonlight was streaming through the window. I saw that old woman, Old Ahkiiqua we called her, standing naked in ribbons of light." Grandma would pause to see if I was paying attention.

"Then what?" I'd ask as if I hadn't heard the story dozens of times before.

"I froze. But I couldn't look away. I held my breath. I was scared and didn't want to get caught spying on that old woman. I pretended I was sleeping—but I peeked through a spot between my hand and the blanket."

"Did she see you?"

"I don't think so. Old Ahkiiqua, she climbed onto the windowsill. She had crow feathers tied to her wrists, shoulders, and head, and crow's feet lashed around her ankles." She motioned with her hands.

I stared at my own wrists, imagined them turning into wings.

"Then," said my grandma, "the Old Woman squatted on the edge of the windowsill."

I always shivered at this part, picturing the old woman perched there in the moonlight. Grandma always paused dramatically and I always raised my clenched hands up to my mouth ready to suppress a scream.

"Then..." Grandma said, pausing again, "she turned her head and looked right at me!"

At which point I'd squeal.

"I felt her eyes scorching the air between us. I couldn't breathe. Then, suddenly, she jumped from the windowsill. Spread her arms and jumped, just like that. I jolted forward as if I hoped to catch her before she fell. But instead of an Old Woman falling to the earth a large black bird flew from the window into the cold night air."

We let that sink in.

"I never again stayed at Elsie's house."

"I wouldn't either!" I'd yell out.

Grandma would laugh and shrug her shoulders. "That's just how it was back when I was a girl," she said.

I was relieved but also a bit jealous that I didn't have to worry about my friends' grandmas transforming into birds at all hours.

"Tell me again," I'd say, absolutely fascinated by the idea of a little girl's grandmother turning into a crow and flying into the night. "Please, Noko."

My brother has this theory. "We all want to fly," he says.

"No," I say, "some of us want to fly and some of your stupid friends just want to get high."

But I only say that to be a smartass because that's how my brother Fizz and I talk to each other. It started when we were tweeners and hasn't stopped since.

Anyway, despite my snarky remark, secretly, I believe him. We all envy birds and if we didn't know the story about the guy plunging to his death after flying too close to the sun, we'd all be constructing wings in our basements, garages, or attics. We all want to be Superman or one of the other flying superheroes, not necessarily so we can do good deeds or wear tights and capes—though I've often wondered why my brother and his friends didn't recognize a cross-dresser when they saw one—but just so we could stick our arms out and zoom off to impress the poor flightless schmucks standing there with their hands shielding their eyes as we set out to turn back time by flying backwards around the earth.

"Hey, suckas, see ya yesterday!"

And who doesn't want to have a personal jetpack to strap on their back? Just every kid who ever watched the Jetsons, that's who.

"Okay, Mom, I'm off to visit Auntie Pat..." you could call out as you slipped your jetpack over your shoulder on your way out the door. "...in NEW ZEALAND," you'd say real casual-like.

"Okay, honey, but it's Aotearoa. Don't be late for dinner," she'd say without even looking up. "We're having moose-meat stew."

"Yes, Mom."

"And wear your helmet."

"Yes, Mom."

"Oh, and pick up some poi on your way home, okay? Your Dad loves that stuff—that's what I get for marrying a former US Marine stationed in Hawai'i."

"From the place in Hilo?"

"Please."

"Sure thing, Mom," you'd say as she mumbled something about the Native Hawaiian sovereignty movement and the irony of falling in love with an American—an American MARINE for gawdsakes.

"See you at 6:00."

———

I love birds. Except for crows. I don't know what it is about crows. Maybe it was my grandmother's story or Old John Rabbittail's stories about crows, I don't know. But they get on my nerves. You can't go a damn place without a crow screeching from somewhere at you, sticking their beaks in your garbage, stealing your food, or laughing at you when you're skinny-dipping with your boyfriend. Damn crows!

John Rabbittail said that crows were the original colonizers. I thought it was a bit harsh but he was always saying provocative shit like that just to get people's attention.

"Yep," he said pushing his lower lip over his upper until his face seemed to be in danger of being swallowed by itself.

"Colonizers of the avian world," he continued, releasing his jaw. "They go anywhere, steal the eggs of other birds, don't seem to belong anywhere, take what they can get, and then some of them move on to do the same thing somewhere else. Buggers."

"Oooh-kay," I said in that long drawn out way that suggests you think the other person is a nut.

"And they don't know enough to shut up!" He slams his mouth shut like he's just made a very important pronouncement.

Well, actually I had to agree with him on that. They do screech and carry on. Hmmm...I thought. Old Rabbittail might be on to something. And if crows weren't my favourite birds as a kid they were certainly plummeting after John Rabbittail put his two-cents worth in the mix.

"Yeah," I said. "Damn loudmouth thieves!"

That, I believe, was also the beginning of my burgeoning political consciousness.

———

So, here's a typical conversation between my brother and me:

"If you don't see that new anime film by Miyazaki, you're stupid," Fizz says completely out of the blue.

"Hey, remember when Loretta and I each bet you a toonie you couldn't eat a bowl of our homemade wasabi ice cream?" I respond in typical non sequitur.

"You're stupid."

"...mint ice cream and half a bottle of creamed horseradish..."

"It's all hand-drawn."

"...and you were such a greedy brat you got to the next-to-last spoonful and got the heaves..."

"It's the best animated film ever," Fizz says. "He's the master."

"I've never seen anyone turn that colour of green."

"I hate you."

"So, because you didn't finish it, we didn't pay you." Then I laugh. "Do you want to go to the early show or the late show?"

My brother looks at me, rolls his eyes, and says, "Rub salt, Jackass."

"Mom likes me better," I say.

"You pay," he says.

———

Do you know what it means if you fly in your dreams?

I used to date this guy, Junior Odemein, and he studied dreams. He was always telling me what his dream was about the night before and what it meant. This guy remembered everything in his dreams. I mean everything. It'd take him half an hour to describe one dream to me. The colours, the sounds, whether the water was hot or cold, how many windows in the building, on and on. That's when I became a coffee addict. Sitting in Coffee Culture with Junior after school listening to him talk about his dreams then ramble on about every friggin' nuance of each symbol, while I'm downing cup after cup of java with double cream. I didn't know then that I was lactose intolerant—I blamed the gas on the fact that Junior was a windbag—I claimed it was contagious.

But, in fact, I learned a lot from Junior. Not just about dreams either if you know what I mean. He had the hardest, best-defined abs of anyone I've ever met. Abs you could wash clothes on! Abs that could hold your filing! Abs that could save the world! Abs for world peace!

"In the dream lexicon," he says, "most of us speak a similar symbolic sort of language. Although some symbols have cultural meanings and some have personal meanings, kinda like dialects and accents."

"I'll have a large coffee, double cream," I say.

"The idea is to understand your own dream language..."

"Better give me an apple fritter while you're at it," I tell the uniformed kid behind the counter. That was also the year I gained five pounds. Of course that was before I read a book that told me that I can't eat wheat or I'll gain weight because I've got a hunter-gatherer metabolism.

"What about abs in dreams?" I say. "What do rock-hard abs mean?"

Junior got me interested in a lot of things. Dreams being one of the few I can talk about publicly. He told me that flying is one of the most positive things that can happen dream-wise. And the more you're in control of the flying, the better. Like if you're in a plane but someone else is piloting it, that's good, but if you're the pilot, it's better, and if you're the bird, the plane, or Superwoman flying around completely under your own power, it's the best.

Junior told me that this psychic poet guy he knew told him that you can learn to fly in your dreams and that you can do all sorts of things then, like flying into other people's dreams, astral travelling, and all that.

I was like, "Yeah, right. As if." But actually, that was just to cover up the fact that I really, *really* wanted to fly and even flying in dreams sounded pretty damn cool. I started paying way more attention to my dreams after that.

Besides getting me interested in the dream-world, Junior made other long-term impressions on me. The sight of firm, de-fined abs still makes me break into a 49er. *"Darlin' with the rock-hard abs, please dance over this way honey..."*

And when someone in my dream has a six-pack, I know exactly what that means. *"...And take me home in your beat-up truck, waya hey-ya, hey-ya, ya-hey, OH!"*

For four years I tried to fly. After three years I could tell myself to walk in a certain direction in my dream and usually my dream self would do it. I could jump, skip, bounce, hop, and hip-hop...hell, I could spin on my head. But I could not fly.

I got so desperate and impatient I thought about enlisting in the air force—but sanity prevailed and my girlfriend Roxy and I laughed for weeks about that.

"You, in the military," she said. "Wee-shtat-ahaa!"

Roxy suggested I take flying lessons. Since I didn't have $10,000 laying around or a rich terminally ill uncle in the cupboard, I gave up on that idea pretty damn quick. Then I thought I could take skydiving lessons. I'd get to be in a plane, which I thought sounded cool, and hurtling to the earth with a parachute strapped on my back would be close to flying, eh? The big problem is that I'm deathly afraid of heights. So, getting me up in a small airplane then expecting me to willingly jump out of it was a bit unrealistic. Roxy suggested hypnosis. Junior thought perhaps yoga and meditation would help and if that failed I could pull out the big guns and start doing sweats to help me overcome my fears. My brother gleefully offered to go up with me to give a helpful push.

"I'll even pay my own way," he said.

"Screw off."

"The end of your nose wiggles when you talk," he replied.

Reflexively, my hand touched the end of my nose. Bad idea. Very bad.

"...Rabbit-kwe."

"Sally says kissing you was like kissing her little brother..."

"It'll be worth every penny," he said giving the air a shove with his two hands.

"...except he smells better."

I tried the hypnosis first. It didn't help me overcome my fear of heights but I did lose five pounds and stop smoking so maybe my mind was wandering while I was staring at the necklace moving back and forth in the hypnotherapist's hands.

Yoga was also good. I lost another five pounds doing that and my flexibility was the best ever. Junior was thrilled, to say the least. It's truly amazing how impressed men are by women who can bend and contort their bodies without falling over or getting a cramp at an inopportune time. Prior to yoga, I had no idea that flexible girls have more fun. A whole new world opened up to me.

But I still broke into a sweat at the thought of jumping from a moving plane.

Despite my brother's constant offers to push me from a plane or tall building, I never did manage to skydive. However, I did start doing all sorts of things to overcome my fear of heights. Meditation, automatic writing, sweats, fasts, support groups. It dredged up all sorts of things I hadn't expected. Did you know that anger is a mask for fear? And that fear covers up shame or hurt? I felt like a bloody onion and, although I began to recognize that the way I teased people was really a symptom of my deep-seated fear of abandonment, after a year I wasn't any closer to skydiving or to astral travelling which is what had started it all in the first place. I was becoming discouraged, in a very non-judgmental, compassionate sort of way of course.

Junior and I broke up around then.

"You're too angry," he said. "I can't talk to you anymore."

"Shut up," I said. "Maybe I'm angry because I am sick of listening to your endless boring monologues about your stupid freaky dreams!"

"Quit projecting," he said. The guy read way too many self-help books.

"Project this," I said, flipping him the bird.

Soon we were both furious. So, of course, we had amazing sex, got back together, then broke up again a couple of days later just to make the breakup official.

Looking back I think we were just looking for different things at the time. Junior wanted a tantric sex partner with an uncanny ability to hang on his every word. I wanted a man who would shut up and teach me to fly. A man with rock-hard abs.

"Way-hey-ya ya-hey-OH!"

It was about that time I decided that the most logical thing to do was to date a pilot. 'But of course,' I thought. 'I can solve my fear of heights, get free flights and maybe an occasional flying lesson, and get some much-needed nookie all from the same source.' All I had to do was find a gorgeous, single bush pilot with a six-pack, and I'd be all set. The perfect plan!

Of course I had no idea how difficult it is to find a single, gorgeous bush pilot—with or without killer abs. Even commercial pilots don't have to be hunky any more. And which idiot at the airlines decided that flight attendants now need to be funny, not spunky? I mean, every time I fly now they're carrying on like they're auditioning for a spot on Last Comic Standing. "Hey, Ladies and Germs, welcome aboard. A funny thing happened to me on the way to the airport...." Suddenly, Junior's prattle about dreams didn't seem so bad.

But I am nothing if not persistent.

"Stubborn," Fizz says, "you are a stubborn pain-in-the...."

Amazing how a sturdy flick of the nose helps my brother to see me differently. And when he's bent over holding his nose like that, well, call me sentimental, I see him differently too. So, it turns out those Zen vegan optimists are right—it is all good.

Needless to say, I spent a long, frustrating couple of seasons hanging around the local airport and flying school trying to fulfill an unattainable dream.

Then, one day I walked into the restaurant in town and there he was.

Jesse Jones.

I stared at him until he noticed me then I spent the rest of the time ignoring him. (I read a book one time that told women that showing interest then playing hard to get is the sure-fire way to get a man's attention. Sadly, it's true!) I ignored him so vigorously that I have never examined a meal as closely as I did that day. Did you know that if you stare at each item of food before you put it in your mouth, it tastes better and you eat less? Apparently that is called "mindful eating" and it's very popular amongst people who meditate and want to be thin or have lost their money and don't want to be seen at the local food bank. Them and people who are paranoid about being poisoned or who are trying really hard to ignore the new talent at the table across from them. Mindful eating: yet another bit of useful information from my time with Junior. Yep, I stared and stared and slowly chewed and chewed and, I must confess, a toasted egg sandwich and fries never tasted so good. Seriously. Even the ketchup seemed particularly red and delicious. Mindfulness really works. Try it.

So anyway, here's Jesse: six feet tall, short spiky black hair, jeans, clingy orange biking shirt, big gleaming white smile, dark smouldering eyes, luscious lips, wide shoulders, thin waist, flat Indian ass, and skin a girl just wants to dive into. And underneath those clothes, the promise of abs so defined you could scrub clothes on them.

Here's me: eyes popping out, heartbeat quickening, jaw dropping. Smitten.

Okay, so I finish eating my sandwich and fries and sip the rest of my coffee while Natasha Reid, the kid who dropped out of school at 15 to have her first baby and who, at 21, is now a single mom with four of the little jam eaters, goes to get me my bill. I try to look extremely cool and calm yet thoughtful and important. Like I have very important things to do with very important people yet am grounded and humble enough to savour a simple meal at the local diner. 'What poise!' I wanted him to think. 'So attractive and intelligent and obviously important!'

Now what? I had to pay my bill and leave without seeming aloof or unapproachable. However, jumping across the table and into his lap was out of the question. Something more subtle yet just as stimulating.... I had him hooked, I could tell, but how to reel him in? Damn! Why, oh why do I merely skim through articles like "How to Hook Him and Reel Him In" when reading magazines in the checkout line at Knechtel's? Damn! Damn! Damn! Why must I always be so distracted?

So, there I was. Natasha brought me the bill. I stood. Still deep in thought about how to solve my dilemma, I gathered my jacket and purse then turned to go to the cash register to pay. The problem was, I was so deep in thought I knocked over my coffee cup with my purse, turned to catch it, tripped over my own feet, and fell into The Spunk's table, knocking his half-full (see: I'm an optimist) glass of iced tea into his lap at the same time. He immediately jumped up so that when I looked up at him in that horrified and sheepish yet, I hoped, attractive way to apologize, I was staring directly at his tea-splattered crotch. Then, as the words of The Friendly Giant echoed in my head, I looked up, *way* up. He smiled.

"Oh, uh, hi," I said as cool as ever, "uh, my name is, uh... Pechi."
I stood up and stuck out my hand. At least I had the presence of mind to stand *before* reaching out my hand.

He shook my hand. "Well, hi there Pechi." He grinned. "My name's Jesse."

I grinned back at him. He really was cute. Damn!

"You know, usually when women fall for me it's not quite so literally."

Oh-oh. A gorgeous guy who probably had the abs of my dreams and who teased as naturally and well as members of my own family. I knew right then and there, I was a goner. I mean, if he didn't turn out to be one of my cousins.

"Why do you want to know about Jesse Jones?" my mom asked in that cut-to-the-chase way that mothers have.

"No reason."

"Well, there must be some reason."

"Nothing really."

"Well, a person doesn't just wander around going, hey, who's that person...."

"Yeah, well...."

"I mean, that would be quite strange if, for no reason at all, everyone walked around saying, 'tell me about him" and "tell me about her'..."

"Okay."

"...and they didn't have any reason just, you know, like on a whim, started asking all sorts of questions..."

"I didn't ask all sorts..."

"...who is he? Who are his grandparents? How old is he?..."

"I didn't ask...."

"I mean, who'd have time for anything else except...."

"All right! All right! I met him at the diner in town...."

She kept wiping the counter and let the pause stretch and yawn into a big questioning silence.

Sigh. "I bumped into his table and knocked his drink into his lap."

She gasped. "You didn't!"

"Yes, Mom. I did." She stared at me with her eyes wide and mouth hanging open, hands on her cheeks, like she was imitating the figure in that painting *The Howl*. I wanted to wrap my hands around her neck and squeeze— tightly. "He was very nice about it."

"Humpff," she said. "A lot of people would get mad about that. There they are enjoying a nice lunch and some klutz comes along and next thing they know...."

"I'm not a klutz!"

She turned and looked at me with a compassionate expression that practically screamed, 'Ah, poor thing, she doesn't even know she's an uncoordinated spaz.'

"I was trying to catch a glass that I knocked over with my purse when I was leaving and I sort of tripped and bumped into his table."

"That sort of thing happens to you a lot," she said. Then without pausing she added, "Jesse Jones...let's see, he must be about your age. You must've met him before. I'm sure that when you were kids you and his cousins, Jack and Cole, used to play together. Oh, yeah...he's the little guy you were always trying to kiss."

"Mom!"

"You'd chase him around the yard. He'd be yelling his bloody head off. It was so cute."

Did her joy in tormenting me know no bounds?

"Sometimes Cole and Jack would hold him down for you. You could hear him yelling all the way to the Community Centre!" She paused to laugh. Jack and Cole are my cousins. So, was she saying he was or wasn't my cousin? I had to know. Thank god for her twisted sense of humour. I made my move.

"Jack and Cole's cousin? Is that Denny's son?"

"No! No!" she snorted at me as if I was truly daft. "Denny is Margie's brother. Well, actually half-brother. You see their father was married twice and..."

Good. That meant he was their cousin but not mine. She blabbered on about who was related to whom and totally forgot about embarrassing me with details from my childhood Hall of Shame or with comments about my current physical coordination skills, or lack thereof.

Yep, genealogy. Gets the Oldies every time.

———

"Did you know that a woman fell 3,000 feet and survived?" Fizz asks me in total non-sequitur fashion one sunny early May afternoon.

"What the hell are you on about?" I replied. I had just been telling him about a poem I read by Allen Ginsberg called "Gospel Noble Truths" and was looking for that book of *Essential Zen* I'd found in the discount bin so I could recite it for him when he left-tangented me.

"An airline flight attendant."

I stare at him.

"She was in the bathroom and the plane blew up or something and crashed and she fell 3,000 feet, hit the earth and survived."

"Jackshit!"

"It's true. I read it."

"So. You can't believe everything you read, dum-dum."

"And this other guy fell 1,000 feet and survived."

"From a plane?"

"No, the Space Shuttle. Of course a plane! I think that one's in the *Guinness Book of Records*. I'm pretty sure."

"How can someone fall 1,000 feet and survive?" I asked rhetorically.

Fizz pulled his lips in and concentrated.

"Let alone THREE THOUSAND..."

"Maybe she landed on something soft."

"Like what? A mountain of pillows?"

"That doesn't even make sense."

"It's sarcasm. I mean, when you're slammed into it from 1,000 feet up how soft would anything feel?"

"The guy who fell a thousand landed on snow."

"I wonder how fast they were falling when they hit the earth?"

"At what point does a body fall upwards?"

"What?" My brother is truly weird. Like most men.

"Like a feather. Why do paper and feathers fall up sometimes?"

He had me there. "I dunno. Updrafts? Wind resistance?"

"Does your speed continue to increase as you fall, or do you reach a point where you can't fall any faster?"

"Oh, shut up, Fizz." My head was starting to hurt. How fast *does* a human body fall anyways?

"I mean, why do some things float or fly and other things get smashed to bits?"

The vein in my left temple was throbbing. I could feel it. Buh-boom, buh-Boom, buh-BOOM...

He looked at me rubbing my head and frowning. "Geez, you're grouchy. Maybe you should read a poem about how to stop being such a..."

"Hey, here it is," I said, waving the book in front of him. After I finished the poem he was quiet for a moment.

"Fall down, you fall down," he said.

I couldn't get over it. "Really? Three thousand feet?"

"Yep," he said. "Fly when you fly."

"What are the odds?"

"Jellyroll," Fizz muttered. "Hey!" His face lit up. "Is there any of that cake left from last night?"

The next time I saw Jesse I was sticking my tongue down his throat without the least concern that it could accidentally lead to us having a child who looked like an extra from the cast of Deliverance—except with dark skin. What a relief I tell you. I was free to pursue and be pursued by this man with lustful abandon.

Thanks, Mom!

And, oh yeah, he isn't a pilot. But he is an outdoorsman. He's always out there climbing up the side of a mountain, or dangling in treetops, or something. Climbing, cave diving, ridge walking, paddling, tree climbing. Partly because he loves the physical challenge and enjoys being outside, but also because he is an avid naturalist, hunter, tracker, and protector of the natural world. At first, I thought he was a thrill seeker, looking for the next adrenaline rush. But no, he's one of the good guys.

So, the question is, how did I get from sucking face with Jesse to camping with him?

A series of intricate moves and maneuvers worthy of the Cirque du Soleil. Well, it actually wasn't much of a stretch. You know, one thing led to another, hormones dived into the mix, and before I knew it we were making plans to spend a weekend up the peninsula to do some rock climbing and swimming and uh…stuff. I was hoping for a romantic weekend of mostly "stuff" with an occasional swim and hike squeezed in that we could rave about to family and friends.

What? I mean, did I mention his washboard stomach? Enough said.

Anyway, we decided we'd camp in the Hunting Grounds and hike from there to the bay or the escarpment each day. Presto magic. I found myself one clear summer morning waking to the smell of coffee brewing and eggs frying.

Later that morning we ate cold eggs and drank coffee so strong the spoons disintegrated around the edges. After that we gathered our gear and set off for a few hours of rock climbing. Jesse talked the whole way. It was incredible. He blabbered on and on about rock-climbing etiquette, the protocols, rules, safety issues, precautions...interrupting himself every so often to point out a plant or track or scat to me. Yep, there's nothing like a couple in love hunched over a smelly pile of fox shit to get the old juices flowing.

In fact, Jesse talked so much I totally lost track of time and space and yelled out an order for a coffee with double cream and an apple fritter. I couldn't help it. I was conditioned—like one of Pavlov's mutts. Jesse stopped dead in his tracks and stared at me with one eyebrow raised. Let me tell you, it sure wasn't easy working a Coffee Culture order into the conversation. But not being one to shrink away from a challenge I set off on a course of verbal gymnastics so impressive that if it were an Olympic event I would have taken home the gold. I mean, I don't want to brag or anything, but I was the Nadia Comaneci of this event, except taller. So, after a series of convoluted explanations involving the racist Tim Hortons "No Drunken Indians Allowed" incident in Lethbridge, the impact of the coffee trade on the environment, globalization, multinational corporate irresponsibility, and a brief foray into the problems with GM apples, rates of lactose intolerance in First Nations people, and whether deep frying is partly to blame for rocketing rates of cancer in North America, I think I convinced him that it made perfect sense for me to blurt out "I'll have a large coffee, double cream, and better give me an apple fritter while you're at it."

Sometimes I'm so good, I scare myself!

Trouble was I couldn't stop thinking about that coffee and apple fritter. Jesse kept quizzing me about rock climbing but my heart wasn't in it and neither was my brain. I kept hoping against all logic that we'd pass a coffee shop drive-thru window but apparently they hadn't yet thought to set up portable donut shops in the middle of the bush. Not that I wouldn't be outraged if they did. Of course I would, but my addiction was clearly clouding my judgment at that point. I hate to admit it but if there had been donut shop on our path I would've gotten my order and scarfed it down out back before wiping away the crumbs and starting an environmental protest out front. Call me a hypocrite but at least I know I have a problem and, if there were such a thing, I'd be attending every meeting of CCA (Coffee Culture Anonymous) in the tri-county area.

And no, this isn't a blatant and cynical attempt to grab some of those big corporate product placement dollars. It just happens to be an integral part of the story. After all, I'm not saying it's either a good or bad coffee or fritter or that anyone else should try their coffee or donuts or boycott their coffee and donuts or stage interventions in Coffee Culture parking lots. I'm just acknowledging my addiction and its tragic consequences....

———

"So are you certain you know how to???"

"Yeah, yeah," I assured him. All the while thinking 'hmm... the apple fritters don't have a filling, so why do the blueberry fritters have that jam filling in the centre?'

Again, I ask, why must I get so easily distracted?

We walked for what seemed like hours. Come to think of it, it *was* hours. Finally, we reached the perfect spot of the escarpment for climbing. I could tell by the angle of the sun hitting the rock face and the way Jesse stood there saying "Babe...." Actually I think what he said was: "Babe, this is the perfect spot for climbing."

"Hunh?" I replied. "What?"

"Let's climb. It looks perfect."

"Okay."

As we were preparing our gear he went on and on about the place. "Check out the slope at the bottom, then how it gently curves before going almost 90 degrees. See the small crevices and cracks? I can't wait to get my hands in there."

I stared at him. Was he going to climb it or make love to it? Sometimes I really wondered about this kid. So, I responded the only way I knew how: "Ever sick!"

He blushed. Honest. He did. Maybe he was thinking about that story I'd read to him the other night about a man and woman who have sex with a stone statue of a fertility god. Or maybe he really was secretly turned on by the idea of putting his hands into the moist, dark crevices of the rock.

"Yeah, well..." he said in an extra husky voice, "we better get moving, Sweetie." Then he smacked me on the ass.

So naturally I plowed him a good one on the shoulder. "Hey! Get away from me you rock lover! Geeez!"

Again, he blushed.

Damn, he was cute! I swear I wanted to rip his clothes off right then and there and climb him.

———

As we put on our harnesses and assorted other rock-climbing gear that I didn't even know the purpose of, I couldn't take my eyes off of Jesse. I was hypnotized by the way he moved, as if he was a part of the land and somehow moved in rhythm with the earth, and wind, and sun. He had a gracefulness I'd never fully appreciated until that moment.

Then it hit me. I'd once read about a star called V838 Monocerotis that suddenly became 600,000 times brighter than the sun and for a moment was the brightest object in the Milky Way. In that instant I knew—Jesse was the most brilliant star in my universe. I was in love.

I suppose I should've been paying more attention to the rock I was clinging to, to the earth below, and to the forces of gravity. But I let my mind wander for just a moment and fell into the gap. First in that sort of Zen Buddhist kind of way where your mind goes blank. I let go. Then I actually felt myself falling.

Hey, I thought, as I felt the air rushing past.

It was beautiful. I blossomed, throwing light echoes into the sky. Then my shoulder slammed into the earth and I blacked out. When I came to I was in Jesse's truck. I knew it was Jesse's truck because even as he careened along dirt roads to rush me to the hospital he had his motivational CD on. "You, yourself, are the only real obstacle keeping you from achieving all that you've ever dreamed of…." I groaned, but not because my body ached like it had just been slammed into the earth from 30 feet up—which it had. It was a reflex I'd developed upon hearing those damn CDs.

"Baby," Jesse said. "I was really scared you were in a coma or something."

"Shut that damn thing off!" I yelled through my swollen face.

The rest of the drive was unusually quiet. But I reached out and managed to touch Jesse's hand. His breath stopped and he cleared his throat. He stroked my bruised and scraped palm gently with his index finger. Then he let my hand rest on his.

I don't know how fast we were travelling but inside the cab it was quiet and still.

When we got to the hospital there was a whirl of noise and activity that crashed and beeped until the cacophony seemed to meld with the rhythm of my throbbing head and ragged breathing and Jesse's footsteps running alongside my gurney—until it all turned into a heartbeat that seemed to encompass the entire universe. Everything seemed joined by that one pulse. I felt a tear fall from my eye and my body soared through the corridors, through the emergency room doors, and out into the clear cerulean sky, soaring higher and higher until even the clouds became a distant memory.

When I woke three days later, Jesse was sitting by the bed. He had one hand resting on my arm and with the other he was drinking a coffee, double-double no doubt.

"Hey," I said. My voice was hoarse and scratchy—as if I hadn't used it in a week. Which I hadn't.

He jerked forward and spilled coffee down his chin.

"I want some."

He jumped up, spilled coffee on his pants and leaned over me breathing his milky coffee breath in my face. "Sweetie," he said. His eyes were like two small cups of espresso about to overflow.

He kissed me and started to shake.

"Jesse?"

"Yeah?" he sniffed.

"I know it now."

He lifted his head from my shoulder and looked at my face. "Know what?"

I can fly.

whale song in riverain park

KISS. WE MEET IN THE FIELD BETWEEN RIGHT AND WRONG.
pull blanket overhead. laugh in this world we create. shouldered
hills, knee mountains, backboned plains, rib-caged valleys. land
of filtered sunlight. cocooned like two children sharing a secret.
touch me here. kiss me there. lips and fingertips. right here. he
smells of musk and cedar smoke. i sniff the air in the hollow of his
collarbone. he blazes wet trails down my sternum. we shapeshift.
a snake swallowing its own tail. O. oh, yes, he says. O. oh, yes. yes.
yes, i say. this world is blue. it churns and rolls. i stretch myself
over him. back against chest. his arms, my waist encircle. he licks
my ear. i giggle, elbow him. he tickles the back of my knee. i roll
over. nose to nose. hey mister. he looks at me with wide eyes.
now you've done it, i growl. he flashes me a sheepish pout. i've
been a naughty boy. he winks at me. no, i want to tell him, you're

beautiful, a beautiful, beautiful boy. instead, i place hands on either side of his face. i'm gonna kiss you till you're a mound of quivering jellyfish at my feet. your lips will get numb first, he says. wanna bet? sure, he laughs, either way, i win.

———

we walk hand in hand through the park. come here, he says, i want to show you something. i've already seen it, i joke. i told you, i say pretending to placate him, it's big. ha ha, he says pushing against my shoulder with his. okay, okay, it's *really* big. biggest ever. that's true. he puffs up his chest. whales look at you with envy, i say. who can blame them? he says, look who's beside me. i smile. *sweet talker*. girl, you ain't seen nothin' yet, he says, pulling me towards a small circle of evergreens and birch in the middle of the park. he ducks and holds branches aside. i walk into the midst. a blue blanket is spread out in the centre. he sits down reaching his hand up for mine. i told you already, i tease, it's *really* big. it's so big it makes the cn tower feel inadequate. get down here silly, he says pulling me towards him. he lays on his back, and i do likewise. temples touching we stare upwards. do you see them? he asks. and then, i do. three red tobacco ties in the highest branches. how did you...? there's one for you, one for me, and one for us. i stare at them one by one. say a prayer for each.

after a while, i roll over hugging his midriff. listen to the drumming. hey, he says, get on your own side. how about you get on my side? i'm always on your side baby. ah, my hero, i say putting a hand to my heart dramatically. whatever, he says, nudging and pushing at me playfully. now get *off* me. get *off* you? i never thought i'd hear you say that. oh, you must have me confused with some other guy, he jokes. now, you're gonna get it, i say, sitting on his chest. about time, he says. i pin his wrists with my hands. i'm gonna lick your whole face for that one, beluga boy. oh yeah, you and what army? he says, narrowing his eyes. oh, you want a bunch of soldier boys licking your face? the more the merrier is my motto, he says. dreamer! a man is nothing without his dreams, he says. i am about to ask him which fortune cookie he stole that from but decide licking him would be the better response. i lean down. he wiggles like a fish in a net. in the ensuing melee i, somehow, lick his eyeball. for a moment our eyes are full moons. we collapse into laughter. a gull screeches. ever sick! he says. i was aiming for your cheek. yeah, right—in that case, remind me never to go hunting with you. but you moved! you would too if you had that tongue coming right at you, he says. hah, i'd think it was the tastiest thing i'd ever seen. geez, i hope you flossed and listerined, he says blinking. yeah, i say, the human mouth is *teeming* with bacteria. great—i'll probably be the first person ever to get gingivitis—*in his eye*! have fun explaining that to your doctor, you pervert, i say, laughing. but i was framed! we both know you're the kinky one. well then, i say, while we're here... i unbutton his jeans. hey, he says, someone might see us. we'll get under the blanket, i say, tugging at his pant leg. they might hear us. we'll be quiet. what if... he says, pulling the blanket out from beneath us.

oh, shut up and kiss me.

---

he's right. my lips *are* numb, but i can't stop myself. not until i have kissed every inch of his body. i kiss his outer thigh and work my way to his ankle, his foot, his toes and up the inside of his calf, his knee, his thigh. the higher i go, the harder he gets. i move slowly. we hear a man and woman talking. their voices get louder. the louder they get, the more he squirms, the slower i go. he clenches and unclenches the blanket in his fists. soon voices fade into the distance. i move slowly upwards. so, so slowly. blowing softly on the small hairs at the top of the inside of his thigh. he places a hand on the back of my head barely resisting the urge to guide me. i move higher, letting a few strands of my hair brush across his shaft. with one swift motion he pulls me up and rolls onto me, pushing his hips into mine. i ache for him. you make me so wet. how wet? as the ocean. he hangs over me, a blue whale rising from the depths, then bends to kiss my forehead. hey, i tease him, someone might... sshhh... he says, raising one hand to his mouth and placing a finger over his smile. i wrap my legs around his back, run my hands along his spine. he dives into the ocean. waves roll across my belly.

right now, he whispers to me, whales are crying with envy.

Chloe

THE PEOPLE HUNCH IN CORNERS, IN DIRT-STREAKED JEANS
that are a little too big or a lot too tight, old baseball caps—trucker
caps before they were worn by celebrities, stained Starter caps of
losing teams—and scuffed-up shoes, their dull fish eyes peering
into the night. Alistair slows the car; I hear the intake of breath
between his teeth, low and slow. He raises his hand, points his
finger like a gun, pretends to shoot them one by one. I know his
stomach is a huge, hard knot. The small car fills with the stench
of their misery and his howling despair. I roll down the window
slightly just to feel the air blow the hair at my temples.

 "No," I say.
 "But it's so fucking awful." He nearly chokes on the words.
"I know."

"They'd be better off than living... like this." He angrily waves his arm at them, at the street, at the dirt and decay and squalor.

"C'mon," I say. "You don't know that."

"Oh, yeah?" he says, his voice rising. "And how will it end? Choking on their own vomit in some rat-infested alley? Beaten and left to die? Frozen on some roadside? Or picked up by some freak who does whatever the hell he wants...."

I hang my head. It's true—we don't know how much worse it may get for any one of them.

"But you can't know what joys they have in their lives. Who loves them. Or where they're headed. This may be just a stop on the way to some other life in some other place. It may be the rock bottom they have to hit before they turn their lives around. It may lead to joy. Or freedom. Or... maybe redemption."

He sighs.

His knuckles clench the steering wheel. He presses a little harder on the gas. I close my eyes, for a moment I dream of girls laughing in sunlight. Feel the night air flowing across my temples. Think of my friend Josie rubbing my temples the night she stopped by for a drink and saw my jaw was frozen by a cold concrete rage that set the muscles tighter and tighter until I could barely move and was blinded by the bright white of pain. I'd lost the baby months before but some nights I'd find myself frozen like that, like some grotesque statue, sitting for hours in the darkness, my head pounding, too angry to move. Afterwards, I'd be scared by the way it consumed and immobilized me and would burn cedar to clear the anger from the room. That night, Josie rubbed my temples, massaged my face, held my hand in hers, and slowly,

slowly chipped away the concrete until it all came crumbling down and I cried myself to sleep. When I woke she was sitting quietly with my head in her lap, stroking the hair on my forehead as if I were a child waking from a nightmare. I knew that she had helped me break through that something, whatever it was, that had such a hold on me. I knew that anger would never again hold me in its tight grip.

As we drive, I try to count the people we see so that when I get home I can smudge and say a prayer for them. Often there are too many to count. Sometimes I count only the ones with the shopping carts. Or only the ones sitting down. Or only the ones sleeping or passed out.

Under his breath I hear Alistair swearing. He's thinking of his sister. There's nothing I can say to him. None of the stock words of comfort. We both know it's not okay. That it'll never be okay. That she won't be coming home. Won't be found. And if by some bizarre twist of fate she ever does return it'll be in pieces even if she's still breathing. The dying won't stop. The killing won't stop. The neglect won't stop. The losses will continue to pile up. No good will ever come of it. We'll never know if he could have saved her. Somehow. If there was some bit of magic that could have kept her safe. The what-ifs are acid. They burn, wound, and fester. We scratch at them. Bandage them. But they are always there. Eating away at him and, sometimes, like some sort of contagion, eating away at me too.

I want to kiss his mouth, long and deep. Not because it'll ease his mind but because for a moment I want us both to remember that there is love and tenderness even in this stinking cesspool at the pit of this writhing city.

The street lights flash by. Down every alley I see people dragging their legs, stumbling into doorways, arms strewn over each other's shoulders or raised in fists, mouths yelling, others slumped against each other, sitting on the curb in pairs, or standing in small groups, hands jammed in pockets, eyes darting, watching, always watching, backs to the wall, or passed out on sidewalks, in doorways, covered in thin blankets, lean Boxer and German Shepherd mixes with studded collars and grease-stained handkerchiefs tied around their necks standing beside them complacently as if they too have lost hope of anything different, can't remember a full meal, and haven't the energy to run or fight or do anything other than stay by the sides of these stick men and women while the days and nights pass in a blur of sameness.

Alistair's sister was only 12 when she left that house on the rez, swearing she would never go back. "Let me go with you," he begged her as she gathered her few belongings into a hand-me-down knapsack. "Please, Chloe. Please. I wanna go too."

She refused. "No," she'd told him. "You're a boy, he won't hurt you the way he hurts me. You'll be okay."

"But you'll be all alone," he said, staring at his feet. "I could look after you," he said and stretched himself to look as tall as he could.

"Ali," she said tousling his hair, "sometimes it's better to be alone."

Looking back he wondered how she could have been so selfless, so strong, at such a young age.

"Anyways, if we both go they'll come looking for us and we'll be easy to find. By myself I can disappear."

She couldn't have known how true those words were. He wished he'd known then what it meant. Stopped her before she began erasing herself. Their mother's boyfriend started it and he knew in every fibre of his being that some other man with a windigo soul finished it.

Disappeared.

He pulls the Civic over suddenly. Slams it into park and jumps out before it fully stops. Stomps towards the sidewalk. I jump out not knowing what I am about to face but ready to stand by him through whatever might come.

Sometimes he thinks maybe, just maybe, he's spotted her. He'll stare into the face of a haggard-looking prostitute while she halfheartedly lists her skills and the prices. "More if it includes her," she'll say nodding her head at me. Some of them notice the intensity in his eyes and back away from him, ready to bolt or to fight. Worse are the ones who grow limp at the sight, striking a pose of utter submission.

"He's looking for his sister," I'll tell them so they won't be frightened. I want to tell them that his eyes burned like that even when he was a small boy.

"I'm sorry," he'll say. "I thought you might…." Sometimes after talking to them he'll hand them a twenty or, because so many of the women on that street are Native, a tobacco tie. Most take it. I wonder what they do with them. If maybe one day we'll drive down this street and see tobacco ties hanging from every tree branch and door handle. The women gone, their prayers, at last, answered.

Other times he jumps out of the car and slams his fist into the nearest fence, light pole, or door. He kicks over trash bins or runs until he collapses.

I hold him then, wishing I could somehow pull the sadness and anger from his body.

"I should've gone with her," he'll cry sometimes.

"You were just a boy," I say, holding him on those nights he weeps. "If you had, you'd both be gone. She didn't want that. She had enough without the burden of taking you down with her. She wanted you to be free. Please, Al, give her that much."

"I know." Sometimes his body would go limp as he let the anger seep out. Sometimes, instead, the rage would surface. He'd howl. "I should've fucken killed him. I should've beaten that prick 10 times for each time he put his dirty paws on her."

"You didn't need to, his guilt got him. Ate away at him. It wasn't cancer, it was guilt."

"I hope he suffered, the disgusting maggot," he said this time, spitting the words out. "I hope it hurt like hell."

"Alistair," I say. "Don't."

"He died all nicely drugged up, in a hospital room with flowers and my mom holding his hand. Holding his filthy hand. While Chloe...oh, god...god..."

I close my eyes. Inhale deeply.

"...and all alone..."

I feel him shudder imagining what might've happened to her. His beautiful sister with her long limbs and easy grace.

We never speak of Pickton. The first time a story about it came on the news, Alistair threw up on himself. For days he holed up in his apartment, refusing to see or talk to anyone. When I finally convinced him to let me in, I was shocked. He was thinner and pale. He obviously hadn't slept or eaten in days. There were holes punched in every wall. His phone was ripped out of the wall and in pieces. The TV was also in pieces, either kicked in or smashed with a chair.

He stood at the door glaring at me. With a look that said 'I know you won't be able to handle this rage, this whirlwind of grief.' Daring me to enter.

I stepped across the threshold, pulled him to me, and held his chest against mine. His muscles were tensed and rigid. His arms plastered to his sides as if they were all that were holding him together. I held on. He took a sudden deep breath, put his head on my shoulder, burrowed into my neck, and cried for his sister, for all of the missing women, for their brothers, their families, their friends, their communities, and finally, for himself.

Later we silently cleaned his apartment. Patched the holes in the walls, threw out the TV and broken furniture, packed his suitcase, and went to my house. He never went back. Not even to get the rest of his things. He had brought everything that mattered to him that first night. Everything else I sold or gave away before returning the key to the landlord.

———

I'd known Chloe my whole life. I grew up in the city but spent summers with my grandparents back home on the rez. She was almost three years older and I rarely saw her but something about her made me look for her every time we went swimming down by the docks and every time we went to the store for penny candy.

Mom and Dad wouldn't let Roxy and me go near their house.

"You girls stay away from the Jackson place," they'd say.

"Okay."

"We mean it."

"Okay, okay. Sheesh," we'd say.

"And don't ever go in even if they invite you. Just tell them you have to come home."

"But why?"

"Yeah, why?"

"Just because. Promise."

"Okay, okay, we promise."

We were dying to know why we couldn't ever go inside their house. It looked pretty much like every other house on the rez. Not as nice as Nokomis and Mishomis' place but not as bad as some. "What happens in there?" we asked each other. Late at night, when we were supposed to be sleeping we'd chatter in the dark. Make up elaborate stories of the kind that only a seven and eight year old could invent.

Babies buried in the backyard.

Naked ladies with pouty lips posing on the couch like we'd once seen on the cover of a *Playboy* magazine poorly hidden under one of our older cousin's beds.

Frankenstein-type experiments in the basement.

Rats as big as dogs.

It was the not knowing that scared us most. But we knew Chloe and liked her. There was something sweet and vulnerable in her even though she was faster and stronger than most of the boys and could spend hours swimming on the rare days she wasn't called home right away. She'd dive and splash, laughing and shaking her hair. She was tall and lean, with long sandy brown hair and hazel eyes that sparkled like sunlight hitting a crest of waves. Her little brother, Alistair, was stockier and thoughtful with a mop of curly black hair and black eyes that were fired with an intensity uncommon in such a young boy. He never strayed far from his sister and no matter what he was doing I noticed that he'd look for her every few minutes. If she was smiling, he'd smile then return to what he was doing. If anyone approached her or she looked at all sad or like she needed help, he was immediately by her side. We figured that maybe he did this because, for someone so graceful and fluid in the water, she was really clumsy. At least, she always told us she was clumsy when we asked about the bruises.

She loved to swim and to wander along the beach looking at stones and shells, bits of driftwood, or pieces of glass worn smooth by the sand and surf.

Then one day we met Tom, her "stepfather." We were walking on the road near the dock, singing and telling silly jokes when he walked towards us. Roxy and I both took a step back. I'd never felt my hair stand on end before but at that moment I felt a strange sensation on the back of my neck.

"We have to go home now," I told Chloe. I hesitated, instinctively not wanting to leave her alone with him. It was one of the few times we'd played with her when Alistair wasn't hovering nearby. He'd been sent out on his uncle's fishing boat and wouldn't be home until the next day. When Chloe saw the man walking towards us, the light went out of her eyes.

"Come and have dinner with us. Our Nokom won't mind."

She sighed. "I can't. I'm not allowed."

"Please," Roxy and I pleaded. "C'mon." Chloe looked so sad. Like a balloon with a small tear in it.

She nodded her head slowly. "I can't."

I wanted to take her by the hand and run. Feel the wind rushing through our hair as we ran farther and farther from the shadow of the man drawing closer.

Instead, I grabbed my little sister's hand and we turned for home leaving Chloe to face the dark, looming presence of that man by herself. I wanted to be home, laughing in my grandmother's kitchen, eating fish and potatoes. Yet, with each step away from her my feet felt heavier. I remember stopping and turning back to wave. Chloe was standing in front of him, her head hanging. She seemed wilted as he took her by the wrist. I still see her, a silhouette walking into the sunset pulled along by the hulking shadow of a man with spider eyes.

When we met again years later at a Friendship Centre social on the eastside in that faraway city, Alistair became my self-appointed protector. Most people assume we're simply lovers but this is a love they cannot understand. Even I don't try to understand it. Have learned not to question it. It is what it is. That's all.

He stayed with me a few weeks after I rescued him from his smashed-up apartment then he moved into an apartment across the street. It comforts both of us to be close. In the between-times, between searches, we play chess, eat pizza at midnight, impersonate people from back home, feed each other scone and fry bread, make dreamcatchers from whatever we can find in the neighbourhood, sneak out to matinees, make up 49ers, talk about our dreams of children and log cabins back home on the bay, and enjoy the beauty of this place. During those times he smiles and laughs. Sometimes it's almost like he forgets there is anything more to want in life. At those times I wish I could capture him like that and show him to his other self, the one that patrols Hastings Street's back alleys. As if somehow that would make all the difference, and life could happily move forward. If only he could see the world without the image of his sister's face haunting his every day.

We have our own separate lives too. He likes motocross racing. I hate the noise and get bored. He can spend hours in front of the TV playing video games. I can stay up half the night watching musicals and eating black licorice. He believes a phone is purely practical and uses as few words as possible to get the information he needs before hanging up. I think that long-distance rates are a whole lot cheaper than a plane ticket. I love to dance, go out for dinner, occasionally drink too much wine, and flirt. He rarely dates.

He says someday he'll get married and have a family but until then he wants to keep it simple. We both know it means he needs to be able to keep looking for his sister, to spend his money searching for her, to save what he can in case he finds her and she needs care or, more likely, needs to be taken back home for a proper burial.

And I keep turning back to her too, like the little girl I once was, moving towards my own life but unable to forget her, wanting to look back and find that somehow she's okay and the darkness around her was just a trick of shadow and light.

Alistair watches over me like he once did with her but more careful now, more aware, stronger, less innocent. He insists on meeting every man I date. Most he tolerates, just barely, but once I saw him tense and tighten his fists immediately upon meeting a blue-eyed man I barely knew and was supposed to leave to have coffee with moments later. I'd had to make an excuse—sudden migraine—and send the guy packing before Alistair became uncoiled and struck. When the door closed behind the guy, Alistair simply said, "Don't see him or accept his calls. If he gives you any trouble, tell me right away and I'll deal with him."

"He seemed nice enough," I said, somewhat fascinated by what had transpired.

"He's not."

"Oh."

"Ruthie?"

"Yeah?"

"You're not mad at me are you?"

"No. I mean, I hardly knew him," I stared at him, I couldn't help it. "I'm just curious. How could you tell? You hardly said two words to each other."

"I just know. I dunno how. But he's got a windigo inside. It's like...it's like I can smell it on him."

Jayjay he liked well enough. Eventually. He viewed all of my boyfriends with the same steady suspicion and, initially, Jayjay was no exception.

"Hey, what's with your friend?" Jayjay asked after meeting Alistair a few times.

"What?" I wasn't sure what he meant. "What do you mean?"

"He's always hanging around, staring at me like I'm a thief and he's guarding Fort Knox."

I laughed. "It's just that he knows what a treasure I am," I joked. Jayjay grins. "Alistair's from back home—we grew up together. He looks out for me."

"Oh." Jayjay was silent. A few moments passed while we sipped overpriced, overly sweet mochaccinos. "That's good."

Gradually Alistair realized that Jayjay would be around for a while and after a suitable amount of surveillance, questioning, and, I suppose, sniffing for traces of windigo, he uncrossed his arms and began to relax. They even went to a few motocross races together and once in a while I'd have to zip across the street to drag Jayjay home from one of their legendary late night Gran Turismo tournaments.

Alistair didn't know I wanted a baby so badly, so soon. Jayjay and I tried for a year but nothing happened. Month after month the blood would come again. Gradually our lovemaking grew more and more tense, heavy with the weight of purpose. Disappointed, the stones of unspoken failure became a wall we had to speak through. In time it took a toll on our relationship and we found ourselves moving further and further from each other. Inch by inch the distance grew until he was falling asleep in front of the TV every night and I was going to bed early so I'd be asleep if he did decide to come to our bed that night. When we did share the bed, sex was perfunctory and joyless.

It was such a mundane way for it to end.

After the breakup, Alistair was there beside me. Unsure what to do other than bring me groceries and tiptoe around the apartment, making tea, and covering me with blankets if I fell asleep on the sofa. He cancelled our monthly searches along Hastings Street

and for a time we didn't talk about her, the sister who lurked in
the shadows of our lives.

Then one day after another day of not eating I stood up too quickly
and crumpled to the floor. Not knowing what else to do he picked
me up and carried me to bed. He sat on the edge of the mattress
holding my hand and rubbed a cool washcloth across my forehead.
When I opened my eyes the look of relief on his face made my
eyes water and I sat up and hugged him. He pushed the hair from
my face and for the first time ever, we kissed. I reached up and
rubbed my hand along his jaw. He closed his eyes and his eyelashes
fluttered. There was something so vulnerable and beautiful in it,
my heart leapt into my throat. I had never before noticed how
long his eyelashes are. I kissed his eyes. His forehead. His cheeks.
His mouth.

We sank into each other's arms. Felt the hard edges wearing away.
Rubbing smooth. Melting. A tidal wave rushed out carrying all
of our dreams and fears and longings forward until our bodies
crashed into each other rising and falling like the tide, pounding
the shores, battering jagged upon our skin, until at last the storm
broke and we collapsed to the floor like two canoes tossed on
the shore.

It was the only time we were together. When I discovered I was
pregnant, I decided to wait three months before telling him. I
counted the days, putting down tobacco at the start of each new
month. One month. Two months. And one week. Two weeks....
I was already thinking of names and rehearsing how I would tell
him when the cramping started and before I knew it, I was alone
again, hugging my empty belly to myself, unable to talk about it
because I could not tell anyone without first telling him. And he

could never know. I was afraid another loss would push him so far down he too would disappear. I hugged our baby's spirit close and prayed she understood.

Sometimes now, on our late night missions down Hastings Street, I imagine her with Chloe, walking hand in hand down the beach, laughing and singing, as the sunlight glows on their skin, and I roll down the window, feeling the breeze flow through my hair.

Touching Sky

IT WAS JUST THAT SHE WANTED TO TOUCH HIM. THAT'S WHAT started it. He had such soft-looking skin, she longed to run her hands over him, rub the back of his hand over her face like she did with silk scarves or buckskin gloves. He was standing in front of her, telling her about gaits, how to mix the plaster, about back-tracking and flehming, and she'd have to put her hands behind her back to keep from reaching for him. Just one touch is all she wanted.

His name was Sky. She saw a sunrise in his smile. She saw a star-bright night in his eyes. When he spoke, she felt as if his voice resonated inside of her. He spoke to her about how birds, animals, and humans had once been able to speak the same language.

She became a hawk spreading her wings over him. Circling.

He had long black hair that he usually wore in a ponytail. She daydreamed about seeing his hair loose, spread out against the sparkling white of freshly washed linens. Smiling as she rode him. His hips bucking and her leaning back and into him, pressing her thighs into his sides. Her smiling back at him and the two of them laughing as he pushed into her. His skin, dark and glistening beneath her golden brown skin. Then she would lie beside him and they would move together like two wild horses running through fields of fire. She would stamp her feet and he would rise up, call to her, then nuzzle her neck before they stampeded into the hills and valleys spread out around them.

"If you touch the inside of the tracks very gently, you'll learn to recognize the feel of them."

She watched him speak as if she were the most attentive, serious student in the group of would-be trackers. All the while thinking how she loved the colour of his lips, imagining how they would feel on her neck, breasts, and belly. Imagined them kissing the deepest, most secret places inside her.

The first day she met Sky at an airport in Calgary, she had noticed how his brown eyes had flecks of gold that turned green when he exerted himself. She imagined herself staring into those eyes as he spread her legs and slid into her. Imagined how hard it would be to look away. Ever.

Sometimes after seeing him she was so hot she'd drive to an ex-lover's apartment, invite herself in, and stay until she was bathed in sweat and the raging fire was left quietly smoldering. The problem was it never went out completely and would flare up at the sight of him. Even hearing the sound of his voice would set a wildfire blazing.

Sky seemed to like that when he spoke she was riveted; like that she watched him watching her; like that when he walked into a room she became a cat ready to pounce; like that even if she seemed not to be looking she knew when he was near. Lightning bolts flew from her body and the air between them became an electrical storm front.

Northern lights reflected on the ceiling.

Solar storms turned the sky red.

At dusk, she sprinkled tobacco, thought of it as stardust, and watched the nights lengthen. She thought about old-time stories of humans and Sky People falling in love. Of women watching the night sky, falling in love, and becoming Star People to be with their lovers in the Sky World.

She watched Sky and knew she was made of starlight.

Sky liked her too, she could tell. He wanted her. He tried not to acknowledge it but she recognized it in the way his body reacted when she was near him. How his chest puffed out slightly. How his eyebrows waggled up and down when she talked. How the pupils of his eyes dilated. She was aware of how he leaned into her when she spoke. How his body coiled when another man came close to her.

It was obvious if you knew how to look. If you could read the tracks and knew how to decipher the story.

She tried to stop herself, to not be too obvious, but she caught herself flicking her hair. Noticed that they stood just a little closer when they talked to each other. She laughed a little louder, smiled a little bit more. Tilted her head, batted her eyes, and touched her hair. A case study in flirting, she thought. A walking, talking cliché. Like everyone is when it comes to love.

With him the world seemed wet and vibrant and filled with light, like a moonlit night in spring, when the sap is running and the spring peepers are singing.

And she couldn't help it. She flirted outrageously with him. She was witty. She was fun. She felt the world roll and purr at her feet. She could do anything. She would try anything. She glowed with a deep golden light. Charm oozed out of her pores, like honey from a honeycomb. It was beyond her control. She felt madly, crazily, alive. She wanted to stand in the middle of Elgin Street and sing his name. She wanted to climb Blue Mountain and hear his name echo back to her. She wanted to walk the Niagara Escarpment and tell every buzzard and crow to cry out his name. She couldn't help it. It was him doing this, not her. It was he who awoke her. It was them, together, who saw sun and stars and moon in each other.

———————

They often talked for hours. He laughed and sang to her. She rhymed off naughty limericks and ranted about this and that colonizing government.

"Don't get me started," she'd say before launching into her latest rant. "Aboriginal people in Canada pay 5 billion dollars in taxes but the total amount the government spends on 'Indians' is only 4 billion...."

He'd join in and hours would pass while they plotted to change the world. They'd tell each other funny stories, give each other glimpses of the dreams they kept closest to their hearts, let each other peek at the failures and heartaches they'd endured. After hours of talking, they would hang up, still with words to say.

"You make me laugh," he told her.

She wanted to throw him on the floor and leave him in a panting, trembling heap. She wanted to Kama Sutra him silly. She wanted him to pin her to the floor, pound her into the earth until she forgot where she began and ended. She wanted to rise up and roll him over, wrestle him, tickle him, then hold his arms down with her calves, sit on his chest and feel him lapping at the sweetest part of her. She wanted him to take her hand in his and place it firmly on his balls while his tongue flicked into her like a bear licking honey. Until she had to have him and lowered herself onto his stiff, hard cock, pushing down, down. Until rising and falling, she became the sun and he became a tree straining upward, reaching for her. Until she vanished into clouds. And he melted into the earth.

It's okay, she told herself. He's an adult. Besides he's gorgeous, healthy, intelligent, outdoorsy, and he's Anishnaabe. How could she not be drawn to him?

"He even speaks Anishnaabemowin!" she told her cuzzie-bro Jesse.

Jesse said, "Good. Maybe you'll learn something other than how to call people rude names."

"Or maybe I'll learn a few more to add to my repertoire," she said, winking.

She tried to imagine what that would be like, to have a lover, a sweetie who was all that AND could call out to her in the language. What would he say? She tried to imagine. Men sometimes said the strangest things to her in lovemaking if they spoke coherently at all. One used to mutter strange things under his breath like "bringing home the bacon" and "suck the headsicle." Another used to repeat the same word over and over—"Burrow!' he'd cry out. "Burrow!" She'd laugh and call back, "Enfold! Enfold!"

What would an Anishnaabe man say in the language? She wasn't sure, but she was damn sure she'd like to find out.

She tried to think of the nicknames he would invent for her. Wondered if he would introduce her as his 'buzgim,' or would he use an English word—lover, girlfriend, partner, sweetie...? She'd always secretly harboured a desire to be referred to as someone's 'sweetie.' Even though it was an English word it was such a Nish thing to say. Her toes curled at the thought of it.

She'd had other lovers, Indigenous lovers from various nations, Black lovers, Asian lovers, lovers who were wonderful glorious mixes and combinations of all kinds.... She'd even thought she loved one or two of these men. But not one, not even the Native ones, had ever called her his sweetie. Long ago, she'd believed she'd only ever have Anishnaabe lovers. She didn't want children who were caught between two worlds the way she had been. Called a 'non-Status Indian.' Not her kids. No way. She wanted to be able to give them that much at least.

But love is not so rational. It doesn't give a damn about racist legislation, *Indian Acts*, Band Membership, or Treaty Rights. And lust is even less judicious.

She'd mostly found herself alone when her Anishnaabe-only love policy was in place. She soon realized that politics is politics and love is love and you can't force yourself to love someone, or for them to love you, because your future children would get Status cards.

"It was a crazy idea caused by the insidious policies of a racist government," she told DJ. Still, she always wished love had worked out that way, and deep down she'd longed for a man who could talk to her in the language. Who would call her his sweetie and make scone for her. Who would dry fish and skin deer and make offerings for her health and safety. Who would sing lullabyes to their children in Anishnaabemowin. She wanted a man at home on the land. Grounded.

Once she had fallen for an Irish-Norwegian environmental activist from Albany. He was thoughtful and beautiful, had the nicest ass she had ever squeezed, was wild in bed, *and* he cared about the land. Unfortunately, he didn't care as much for her and although he could commit to a cause in a heartbeat he couldn't commit to her for more than a couple of months. Funny how he taught people to love and respect Mother Earth but was a throw-away consumer of women.

"Is that a vestige of some overprivileged colonial White guy arrogance that his oh-so-aware self doesn't recognize it for the hypocrisy that it is?" she leadingly asked a Tlicho friend once after the breakup.

"Well, yeah," Simon said. "Plus he's an immature idiot."

And now, kneeling before her, with his hand in an Alpha female wolf track, was the Anishnaabe man of her prayers. She wanted that same hand to reach into her. To know her ridges and hollows. To recognize her by touch.

She could see his nostrils flare, sniffing the air around her.

She caught her breath. She wanted him sniffing and pawing at her. Digging up her bones. Hot on her scent.

Each breath he took hung for a moment in the air before dissipating. Like small smoke signals, she thought. Maybe it was corny, but she liked the image. People in love are sentimental fools, she scolded herself. All the while still watching his breathing.

He smiled at her. "Would you like to feel the track?"

"Megwetch," she said, moving closer to him.

Why couldn't she have met someone like him years ago? Why now? Why him? He would have been going to his grade 8 grad when she was getting her MA at university. He would have been in diapers when she was at HER grade 8 grad. Now, here she was, longing, *dying* to touch him. First with her hands, just her

139

fingertips lightly touching his face. So softly her hand would tremble in passing. Then her lips brushing his cheek before grazing his lips. Her tongue would circle his mouth before tasting the tip of his tongue. Later, her tongue would travel the entire territory of his body, mapping it with taste and touch. She would know the smell of him, the texture of the hair on the inside of his thighs, the taste of him, the size and feel of him in her mouth, resting on her tongue. She would know the friction of him, feel the wetness, reach down to the spark igniting.

She would learn to recognize him with just one touch.

Just one touch. That's all it would take.

One touch to begin the story.
One touch to start the migration.
One touch to seed the rainclouds.
One touch to set off lightning storms.
One touch to ignite the frenzy.

One touch after months spent carefully not touching. They'd gone to great lengths to ensure they never touched each other. As if both of them knew what it would mean. If one so much as brushed past the other or if they sat beside each other and their legs touched for even a moment that small patch of skin would tingle and come alive and they'd move immediately as if they feared one of them would spontaneously combust.

"But Officer," she could hear herself saying, "I only just barely touched him for an instant."

"Winona, maybe you just like the young bucks," DJ teased. "Fresh meat, hey?"

It was true. His youth was a turn-on. She'd be lying if she didn't admit that. But if it were just that she wouldn't be taking her time like this. If it had just been about sex with a hot young body it could've been wham-bam over and done with long ago. But it was more than that. He was precious and beautiful to her. She loved the firmness of his body, smooth tautness of his skin, his ease and gracefulness. His strength and playfulness. His way of seeing the world. It made her feel beautiful too. Rather than feeling old, as some other younger men made her feel, being near him allowed her to both appreciate his youthful energy as well as her own hard-won maturity and calmness. Looking at him, she loved the lines that were starting to etch around her eyes and mouth when she smiled, the stories she was able to tell about her travels, her triumphs, and her losses. She loved the feeling of ripening that possessed her body. She could see how it mesmerized him in the same way that his vigour intoxicated her. She felt more vital and he seemed more serene.

Still, her family would tease her when she brought him home. No doubt.

"So, Win," they'd ask, "how old was he when you were starting high school?"

They'd ask if he had training wheels on his Harley. If she had to cut his meat for him or if his mom let him use real knives like a big boy. They'd call her Demi and him Ashton. They'd yell out things when they drove by like "where's your Binogeeze-Man?" Or they'd do things like buy him a Happy Meal and tell her they arranged for Meals-on-Wheels for her.

Her brother Elwin would put a crib in their room. In the morning they'd ask if the "baby" kept her up all night and her brothers would wink at each other and laugh.

Everyone in the whole community would know five minutes after they arrived and would get in on the teasing.

She wouldn't care. She'd laugh too. It was funny after all these years to find him at all let alone in such beautiful wrapping. Maybe the timing was a bit off, but hey, the universe works in mysterious ways, and all that mattered to her was that those years of searching, then those years of despairing and giving up the search, had somehow finally led to this. This man. This man kneeling beside her, reaching into the earth.

As he kneeled there, showing her how to touch the wolf track, she noticed the skin on the knuckles of his hand, the sparkle of stars in his eyes. She wanted to throw herself on him, rip their gear off, and roll with him in the snow and mud until they had to run, their hearts pounding as they shivered and danced in the cold April air. She wanted to take his hand and run until they couldn't run anymore, then their bodies, spent, gasping for breath, would collapse to the earth and they would rise later, blinking into the sun like newly formed beings. Ready to greet a new day, together. And every time they made love they would reenact this scene, and know there was no place else to run. Nothing to hide. New beginnings stretched before them, like sun reaching across the horizon.

She kneeled beside him. Reached out her hand.

Just one touch, she thought.

Just one.

THE DREAMING
AND THE WAKING

TODAY IS SATURDAY. I'VE SPENT THE DAY HERE IN THE HOSPITAL
in Wigawaykee's room. It's a boring place most of the time. When
it's not it can be frightening. Beeps sounding. Nurses and doctors
running. People weeping. Crying out in pain or in grief. And
your own heart starts racing like you've woken from a nightmare.
Except the nightmare starts after you wake.

"Yeah, I know," my mother says. "He saved you. And we can
never repay him for that. But my girl, you gotta move on. You got
your whole life ahead. He wouldn't want you spending it like this.
Alone. No man. No babies."

The light is too bright. This hospital room is always too bright.
Too shiny. It makes me nauseated.

The walls are a faint peach colour. The sheets and blankets are
bleached white. The bed is metal. The window blinds are white.

The curtains are white. There are prints of peach-toned flowers in chrome frames on peach walls. Peach-coloured chairs with chrome legs stand ready for visitors. Sturdy veneer bedside tables with chrome legs and handles perch on either side of the bed.

I hate peach.

Chrome's okay. Only because when you look at it you can see all sorts of distorted images of yourself. I like that. It passes the time during these long days and nights.

I've been sitting here all day. On this peach chair. Beside this metal bed. Where Wigawaykee lies. Still and silent.

I'd like to be able to say to my mom that no matter what I will continue to do this. That I will be here by his side for as long as it takes. That I have the love and the patience to stand by him. But, despite what my mom says, I'm not sure I do have either the faith or the patience.

I'd like to say I do. I'd like to believe that he will survive this. That one day his eyes will open. That he will see me sitting here beside his hospital bed. That somehow the pain and anger and frustration and fear will have been erased from his spirit. That the walls will have crumbled. The masks fallen free and vanished. That I will truly have forgiven him for that moment that sent us both crashing into lives we never would've imagined. That he'll smile.

I've always been won over by that smile of his. If he wanted to I'm sure he could seduce the stars down from the sky and make them dance for him with that smile.

We've known each other pretty much our whole lives. We were friends when we were kids. His dad was prone to drunken rages. He'd beat his wife and kids. Lock them in the cellar, tie them to their beds. Wigawaykee's sister Zeegwun was only four when their dad locked her in the cellar and she got frostbite so bad she lost the ends of two of her fingers. He was a real bastard that guy. Cruel.

"My dad was a good kid," Wigawaykee told me once years later. "When he married my mom he was a big, good-looking guy, always making jokes and laughing. But when he got back from the war, he'd changed. He wouldn't talk for days at a time. He was drunk every day. That's when he started hitting Mom. By the time Zeegwun was born, Mom was scared of him."

At school we'd share our lunches with Wigawaykee and his sister and sometimes they'd sneak by after school or in the evening and my mom would bathe them and feed them until they couldn't eat any more. She'd hug them and they'd smile shyly. Wigawaykee would sit on my mom's lap and she'd hug him and tickle his neck and tell him how cute he was. He'd laugh and squirm but every time he got the chance he'd be back for more. Sometimes he'd fall asleep in her lap and my dad would carry him home, waking him at the end of their driveway so he and Zeegwun could sneak in.

Poor boy.

Now I look at him and I'd like to believe that he'll awaken and that he'll be strong and whole. But I know he was neither of those things before all of this. And yet somehow I want to believe that he'll smile at me and the pain we carry will melt away. I want to believe that the walls of fear we built, the mountains of pain we pushed up from the centre of our hearts, the raging rivers of lies and demands and betrayals we placed between us will be overcome. I want to believe that we could truly love each other, not only in spirit, as we do now, but that we could live together with that same love in our every day.

And so I hang on. I do what I can to help him heal. I squeeze every last bit of hope from my heart. I sit in this room staring at his face. His beautiful face that is slowly melting to bone.

And I give him bone words. The bones of truth. I tell him ribcage stories. Sing him thighbone songs. I talk to him about the sacred burial grounds inside of us. I read bare-bones poems about forgiveness and love. I tell him over and over and over again "I am your friend, Wigawaykee. N'odaysinawn." I sing to him "k'zaugin...k'zaugin...." I say everything he might need to hear to heal his wounded spirit. I burn sweetgrass for him. Bring him wild roses. Massage his body with healing oils. Place him in a circle of stones.

He sleeps.

"We need our men," my friend Ruth says. "We can't afford to let even one slip away."

"Yeah," I say.

I do all of this because I can't bear to let one go. Not this one.

And I do it because I have loved him my whole life. Because he pushed me into the fire then risked everything to pull me out.

I believe it helps him. And it helps me too.

For a long time after that night we fell, I didn't come to see him. I needed to find my own healing. I went home and laid my wounds upon the earth. Then one day I knew I had healed as much as I would ever heal. I decided to wear my scars proudly.

"Scars are poems of survival written across our bodies," I told my mother.

"Ah, my girl," she said and pulled me close to her. She stroked my hair. "My girl."

I let her hug me until she was ready to let go. "Drive me to the hospital?" I said.

It was liberating in a strange kind of way. It made me feel strong. Bursting with life. That was the first day I brought Wigawaykee wild roses.

"I'll come in with you," my mom said.

"No," I said. "It's okay."

"He's not the same," she warned me.

"I know," I said. "But I need to do this myself." She squeezed my hand and stood in the waiting room watching me until I turned down the corridor to his room.

I walked into his hospital room carrying a handful of wild roses. And the moment I saw him I cried. I wept from so deep inside that all language left me. Sounds I had never made before spewed from somewhere inside me. It was like being turned inside out.

I don't know how long I stood there scattering wild roses at my feet. But some time later I found myself beside his hospital bed. I reached out my hand. Touched his skin. It was like parchment, thin and dry. I touched him again and could smell wild roses. I could smell the scent of him. Of us together. I could feel breath flowing from my mouth and nose. I could see butterflies dancing in my eyes. Bears rising from their winter sleep. I could hear voices singing songs I knew yet had never heard before. I cried out in a language hidden in my blood. A torrent of words broke loose and swirled about us until it seemed we would both be swept away.

In the long hours since then I have begun to write. Keesic bought me this journal in the hospital gift shop. I began writing all of the things I could not say. All of the dreams I could not remember. All of the pain and beauty I could not contain. All of the answers to all of the questions I could not ask.

My cousin Lorene sits with me sometimes.

"Lately, I keep having this dream I never fully remember," I tell her.

She puts down her *Spirit* magazine and leans towards me, her head cocked to the side.

"Wigawaykee is in the dream. We're facing each other, standing up to our necks in water. He is on one side of a river and I am on the other. There's blood running from our ears and mouths and flowing into the water. We call to each other. Something. I can't quite remember. The river runs in both directions. He is pulled one way. I am pulled the other. We struggle against the current. I reach for him. He throws rocks at me. My heart is pounding. There's something I can't remember. Then we're running. Our clothes are soaked. We take off our clothes. There are purple butterflies. The sound of wings overhead. We hold hands. Run until we are no longer touching ground. Our skin disappears."

Lorene reaches out and holds my hand. It is enough. We sit like that for a long time, watching him sleep.

"How long are you gonna pine over him?" my mom asks me. She doesn't know the whole story. She doesn't read the poetry in this place.

I shrug my shoulders. "As long as it takes."

"For what?" she says. "For what, my girl?"

I shrug again. I don't know.

Some days I sit here on this hard chair with my feet propped on his bed. I read stories by Sherman Alexie, Patricia Grace, Gerald Vizenor, and Cherie Dimaline. Or poetry by Giles Benaway, Marilyn Dumont, Pablo Neruda, and Hone Tuwhare. I eat popcorn and sip ice water. Just because it makes me feel good. Sometimes I don't read the stories or poems out loud. I just laugh or shake my head or make little sounds when I read something that strikes me a certain way. But often I do read out loud. Sometimes I do it for the stories more than for him. Because they need a voice to set them free in this place.

Here, in the hospital, I began to tell him stories of my own. Stories about life back home. Who's seeing who, who's sleeping with who, who's at school, or who's getting married. Stories about our cousins and their antics on Saturday nights. Stories about birds and graveyards, about the way stones hold history, and about how hair holds memory.

I didn't mean to become a teller of stories. It just happened. I don't know why. Sometimes I try to understand how this happened. All I know is that it has something to do with that moment he turned away.

Today I told him this story:

"One night a man sat in his room. His head was heavy. He sat in the dark thinking about how heavy feelings can be. He loved a woman. A woman with long dark hair and strawberry lips and eyes as expressive as poems. He loved her with his entire soul. But she did not love him. It weighed on him and he grew heavier and heavier until he could barely move.

He had dreams that this woman he loved would kiss him. They would kiss and he would feel himself growing lighter. Together they would grow lighter and lighter until they no longer touched the earth but floated high above the tops of the trees. But on this particular night he could not sleep. He could not dream. He could only sit there as heavy as lead. His spirit was a dull grey stone. His thoughts grew dark like his room. Outside his window he heard a lone wolf howling. The sound filled every space inside him with longing and sadness. He opened his window and sat on the windowsill and heard other wolves responding to the first. He wept as he sat there listening to the wolves. And the burden of unrequited love became unbearable.

He jumped.

As he fell he could hear the pounding of wings. He could feel them inside his chest. It was at that moment, as he was plunging through the night sky, that he wondered if he had loved someone incapable of loving him back, because ultimately he was the one who was incapable of true love."

Wigawaykee didn't react. But I felt a stirring like flocks of songbirds and ravens rising in my chest, and I knew he had heard.

Sometimes it was like that when I was with him. Even before all of this happened I could tell what he was feeling or thinking.

Sometimes we were separated by great distances when it happened. Yet, I knew. I always know, even when I don't want to know. Somehow, we're connected.

"Lorene," I say trying to explain it, "I'm sure it's something as old as the stars and moon—but better than email or text messaging." We laugh.

"Oh, you!" she says, bumping her shoulder into mine.

With Wigawaykee and me it started long ago, sometime after our first kiss, but since that night it happens more frequently and is more intense. It's as if all of the energy he had used to communicate and express himself in other ways now comes directly to me.

So when I told this particular story earlier today I felt a stirring in my chest that stopped my breathing. I was filled with regret and sorrow and love. I wept heavy tears. Then I floated to the top of the room and watched him sleep.

Now I look at him and think how much he has given me. Because of him I am alive. Because of him I am remembering how to laugh. Because of him I am healing. Because of him I honour my ability to survive. Most of all because of him I know I am capable of truly loving someone. He taught me all of that.

So, yes. I would like to believe he will awaken whole and strong. But I know it may never happen. I know that.

And yet I know that love can heal.

Love can heal us all.

KATERI AKIWENZIE-DAMM is a writer, poet, spoken-word performer, librettist, and activist from the Chippewas of Nawash First Nation at Neyaashiinigmiing, Ontario. In 1993 she founded Kegedonce Press to publish the work of indigenous writers and artists. She has written two books of poetry, was editor of the award-winning *Skins: Contemporary Indigenous Writing*, and has also released two poetry and music CDs. Kateri's work has been published internationally in journals and anthologies, and she has performed and spoken around the world.